SWITCHBLADE

ISSUE THREE

Edited by Scotch Rutherford

To Vicki
and Roger !!!

Thanks

- MMMMMMM

Switchblade, Issue Three, Volume One
First Printing, October 2017

ISBN-13: 978-0-9987650-2-0
ISBN-10: 0998765023

©2017 Caledonia Press
www.switchblademag.com

Stories by the authors: © Preston Lang, © Charles Roland, © Eric Beetner, © J.D. Graves, © Ehren Baker, © Morgan Boyd, © Calvin Demmer, © Robert Smith, © Joe Ricker, © J.L. Boekestein , © Richard Risemberg, ©Michael Loniewski

Front cover photo: ©2017 Scotch Rutherford
Back cover photo: ©2017 Scotch Rutherford

Switchblade:
A Screwdriver for the Skin
by Zakariah Johnson

Length of a boar's tusk,

Cheap metal too thin for a grind stone,

Work it with a file but ultimately give up on slashing:

It's a poker, it's a thruster, weighting the pocket by your pecker,

Ready to snit, pop open, flap wings,

A glorified screwdriver for the skin,

Only better by virtue of being banned.

Bought in Juarez, in Chinatown,

Rolled out from a drawer with a wink from the fat freak at the Army Surplus,

It plays, nips like a ferret,

Rolls over hands like water,

Flash here, follow me there, Whoops, you didn't see?

Horns of the buffalo, here, there, the shaggy head shakes,

Threatens from both sides, too quick to see

Denim or leather twirl,

Blades hidden behind your magic capes,

Parry his return in a jacket-wrapped arm,

Snap his at the hilt with a twist as he sinks it in your arm,

And return the favor...

Money's to be made, hinky ones sold to suburban kids with dreams

And no experience against something bigger,

Gap-mouthed youths mesmerized like stupid fish by your flashing lures,

Dollars come out and then they go.

A blade too small to threaten, scare, or bluff,

It's made only for speed and just for being used,

A show you show your foe only when you're pulling it out

Of his chest, for fifteenth time, to wipe it off.

Take his wallet. Ditch the blade. Buy another. They snap so easy,

Unlike tight muscle, walls of the stomach, even skin,

Skin you learn the first time is so much harder to get through,

Skin that's so much tougher to open than you'd ever thought, until it's yours.

CONTENTS

SHARP & DEADLY FICTION

He wasn't dead, but he didn't seem able to get up. She stood watching him struggle to breathe a minute. Then he opened his eyes briefly and looked at her, trying to mouth a word. She caught him one more time—hard in the face with the blunt tip of the putter.

"You think I haven't done it before?" He said, speaking softly now, staring into her eyes. "You think I haven't passed the word, someone disappears?"

The officer held out a hand and Mom shied away from it in a way I'd never seen from her. She was full of surprises that day. I looked at her hands, expecting to see blood, but they were clean with little drops of water in the thin hairs on the backs of her hands.

like I'm outside my own bended knee body, groveling to this pale lump. I could only imagine what my Michelle sees—from inside the car. I loaded the bodies, stacking them like heavy cordwood.

He was a jackal of a man, sharp eyed and baleful. Despite appearing prim in his expensive suit, Harper knew a muscleman when he saw one. Those big, scarred hands the youth kept folded before him were telling enough.

"There's now a bullet with your name on it. Natural progression of the trade," Fred said. "I got one with my name on it too."

Turning around, she saw a figure dressed in black from head to toe. This included a black mask that only had two eye holes. A large blade shimmered under the warm yellow light of the room.

Cowan grabbed Sheppard by the scruff of the neck and slammed him face down into the tofu container. He held him there as he choked, suffocating on the stuff. It was a cholesterol free death at any rate.

QUICK & DIRTY FLASH

You could see it coming from a mile away. In a year Brendan wouldn't be doing pain killers, he would be doing other shit. Bad shit. His money would evaporate, he would lose his place, he would be doing petty crime and die on the street, or end up in jail.

He didn't back off. The punk's head came up to about my nose, so I stood up straighter to make sure he wouldn't head-butt me. Just then a pair of arms came around me and pinned my own arms to my sides.

Reiko's eyes snaked a trail down Helmuth's wounded body. She found a jagged gash in along his leg, raw and open. Her double edged knife probed the shrapnel wound and Helmuth let out a horrible scream of mercy.

He thinks about the three men he's killed along the way, the loud gunshot escorting the bullet to whisper through their brain. A final, rapid lullaby. Sheldon wonders what their last thoughts were.

EDITOR'S CORNER

If this is your first issue of *Switchblade*, then you've joined us at the perfect time. Issue Three is by far the best issue yet. As usual, we continue to deliver the best hardboiled noir fiction the indiependent side of the New York five families of publishing.

If you've been a loyal reader from the beginning, then you're familiar with the work of *Switchblade* veterans J.L. Boekestein, Preston Lang, and Charles Roland—they're back with new short stories and flash. Eric Beetner (of the *McGraw crime series* fame), along with Ehren Baker, Joe Ricker, Michael Loniewski, Robert Smith, Rick Risemberg, Calvin Demmer, Morgan Boyd, and J.D. Graves round out another unique lineup of hard luck tales.

Also in this issue: we're finally taking a stab at poetry. Featuring the edgy, frenetic prose of Zakariah Johnson.

    Scotch Rutherford
—(Managing Editor)

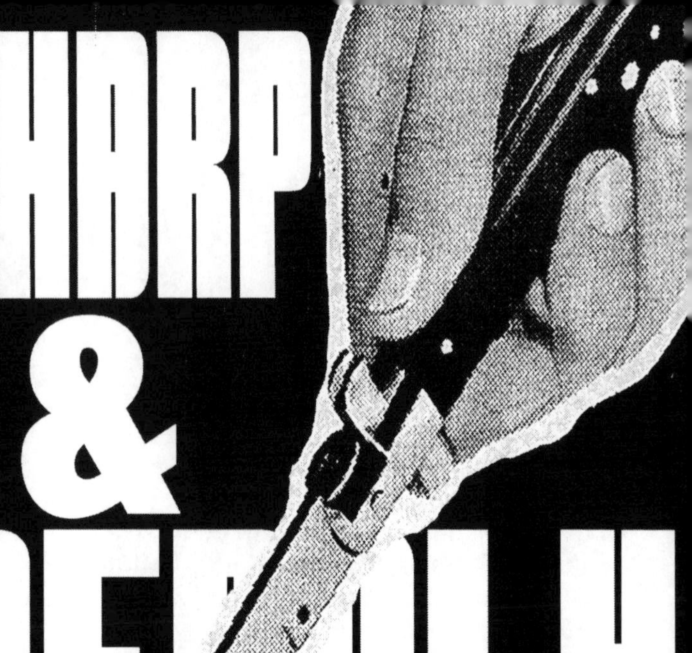

Press It Down

by Preston Lang

There's a button on my booty—press it down, press it down.

The music came out of the boy's phone. Who did he think he was—this smirking, pockmarked teen, blasting his tunes in Kay's kitchen?

"What is this?" she asked.

"It's just a song, Grandma," Emily said. "It's a—"

"Quiet, please."

Kay listened to the vocals then she winced when the rap break came.

"I know it's kind of dumb, but a lot of songs are about butts these days," Emily said.

"What is it? Who does this?"

"It's a guy called Right8," the boy said. "He's the rapper. I think the singing part is some old disco song."

Kay went into the bathroom to splash cold water on her face—angry, disoriented, sick to her stomach.

"Your grandmother really doesn't seem to get hip hop."

"I don't know, she's old."

The apartment was small—one bedroom, a kitchen, a bathroom. The kids didn't appear to understand or care that Kay could hear everything they said.

"She likes classical, you know? Beethoven and Motown and all that."

"Someone's got to tell her that it's not, like, medieval times anymore."

*

Over the next few days Kay heard the song everywhere she went: supermarkets, car radios, ringtones. It blasted out of speakers stuck in the sand on Rockaway Beach, and it seeped out of the earbuds of bicycle deliverymen. At the dental clinic where she worked reception four days a week, Right8 was on

4

television, answering questions on a morning talk show. A handsome, silly rogue, he explained how—*actually*—he had so much respect for women, and clarified just what it meant to press down on that button. *Button on my Booty* was the unmistakable anthem of the summer, and it burned Kay wherever she went.

After work she walked to the library to look through the white pages. Manhattan directory, then Queens, then the Bronx. That's where she finally found him—Arthur H. Ghanbarian. The next morning, an off day from work, she took two trains and a bus to a five-story brick building in North Riverdale. Arthur Ghanbarian—Artie Groove—lived on the third floor. It took him a while to answer the knock. How old would he be now? At least ten years older than she was—an elderly man. He finally opened the door, leaning on one of those three-pronged canes, no recognition in his eyes as he sucked in air.

"Can I help you?"

"I think you can, Artie."

"Jesus." He gave her a full up-and-down. For a second she thought he was going to tell her to give him a spin. "I've got to say—you could look worse."

When Kay was young she'd been knobby and funny-looking, but as an older woman she'd become sweetly quirky—the slightly off-kilter grannie. And she was still trim and fit, unlike Artie. It took him half a minute to get back to the couch and another moment to get his breath back. He'd once owned a record label and two nightclubs, and he'd always dressed well, always seemed to be confidently on the move to somewhere swanky. Now he was a husk in a ratty bathrobe.

"The song," she said. "You've heard it?"

Artie smiled—no shame.

"I've heard it," he said. "This Right8—the rapper? His dad is some finance muckety-muck, his mom was an Ethiopian model. Kid dropped out of Yale to go into the biz. My Aunt Rita is blacker than this guy. No edge, no flow at all. Inauthentic. But what can you

5

say—he hit it big off my song. You heard. He didn't just sample—he rides it. I'll tell you, we did a good job: the bassline bumps, the hook is right in your face. Some of my best work."

He'd lost his physical strength and the huge, unruly wire of hair, but he still had that tongue—quick, abrasive, unapologetic.

"You must be making a ton of money."

"No. I sold the whole catalog twenty years ago. Everything: *Groovedale Academy, Bump it Uptown, Mamma's Got Room to Make it go Boom. Button on my Booty*," he said, pressing down on the coffee table with his left thumb.

"Who bought them?"

"UBC International. Hip hop guys were getting sued for sampling, so UBC went and bought a ton of old records—title and deed. Their artists go through the cuts and take whatever they want. If I still had rights, there's no way they would've used it like they did. So the kid makes millions off my song but only because his label already owned it."

Kay still hadn't sat down. She paced the floor from behind the table, absently picking up the silver putter that stood against the wall toward the window.

"It wasn't your song. It was mine," she said.

"How do you figure?"

"I wrote it. I sang it. You put your name on it."

"You wrote *Button*? You wrote a song about ass?"

"Yes, I did. *Shake your Booty* went to number one. You told me to put something together *along those lines*. I wrote the whole thing in one night."

"First of all: *Shake Your Booty*? K.C. and the God Damned Sunshine Band? *Button* is to that crap song what *Hamlet* is to a fucking Hallmark card. *Button* has depth. *Button* speaks to something real in every human soul."

"And I wrote it."

"You're telling me you wrote these words: *It's ready and it's round, so just push that button down.* You wrote that?"

"Yes."

6

"What do you know about booty? That flat ass of yours? Man, 1977, I was tagging tail all over town. And then you left us all of a sudden."

"I was pregnant and you fired me."

Even after he'd stolen her songs, crediting himself as writer and his wife as singer, she was still willing to work for the man. She just hadn't seen other options.

"Oh, that's right. Pregnant chick on stage, trying to be sexy? Come on," he shrugged. "You had a little girl, right? How is she?"

"She's dead."

"Overdose or something? You were probably a bad mother. What can I say?"

She poked him once with the golf club. Just a little jab in the shoulder, but it hurt the frail, old man. He tried his best to look tough and defiant.

"You're not even on the record," he said. "We had Lana redo the backup track because you missed half the high notes."

"I missed *what*?"

"Lana's voice. My song. Then I sold it to UBC. End of story. If you came here for money, you're out of luck—look at this place. There *was* a nice house, cars, dinners, drinks, some really really nice cocaine, loose cooze on the side. It's all gone now, but *I* had something. I wrote songs that meant something. I was a real part of that moment in time. You stood behind talented people and hummed."

Ghanbarian looked satisfied, like he'd justified his whole existence. He wasn't being cagey to protect his assets; he really thought he'd created all that music. She hit him with the golf club. Hard in the face this time. Then after an uncertain moment, she hit him again—over and over, clubbing at his body, feeling soft spots and hard spots, hitting him until he slid off the couch and stopped moving. He wasn't dead, but he didn't seem able to get up. She stood watching him struggle to breathe a minute. Then he opened his eyes briefly and looked at her, trying to mouth a word. She caught him one more time—hard in the face with the blunt tip of the putter.

7

She left the building, walking along the street, club still in her hand. There was blood on the bottom and a bit up the shaft and also along the cuffs of her jeans, but she didn't think she looked particularly suspicious. A white lady in her sixties could carry a smoking rifle down Broadway without getting a second look. She made her way to Van Cortlandt Park and threw the putter into thick bush up in the back hills. Then she caught the subway and rode to the far end of the line.

*

Two days later, after dinner, Emily surfed the internet, pleased that she was getting a good signal on their neighbor's Wi-Fi.

"Oh, this is crazy," she said. "You know that booty song? The guy who wrote the original got murdered in the Bronx."

"That's horrible. Emily, you have to start going to bed earlier. School starts again in two weeks."

Emily smiled and waved her off—her adorable, ineffectual grandmother.

"Someone beat his head in with a metal pipe."

Kay got two newspapers the next morning before work. They carried nearly identical stories. Arthur Ghanbarian, known as Artie Groove, had been attacked during the morning or afternoon on Tuesday. They estimated that he'd hung on half a day, not letting go until very early Wednesday. Multiple fractures to the skull, a shattered shin bone, extensive internal bleeding. Someone had really taken it out on the guy.

He was a songwriter, producer, club owner, and businessman. The current, number one megahit *Button* was based on a song he'd written and his wife Lana had recorded in 1977. It was the biggest hit the independent label GrooveArt ever had, briefly making it to #67 in the US and charting even higher in Denmark, Belgium, and West Germany. No reason was given for the killing, no suspects, no grieving family. The picture used for the article in *The Post* found him at his most vividly seventies—the loud jacket, the feral, coked-up eyes, and that heavy

8

mound of hair. It was the kind of wild, little story that started to get online buzz. Emily followed it all:

Probably got killed for bringing such sucktastic music into the world.

Guy looks like a perv—writing songs about ass and pressing on ass and whatnot.

Maybe this is a message to Right8. Should not treat women as sex objects.

I'm surprised his skull wasn't protected by that huge, Armenian Jewfro.

*

On Saturday morning just after eleven, the ring came from the lobby—a friend of Emily's probably. But the girl didn't get out of bed, so Kay had to answer it. A low voice came through the intercom.

"Detective Franklin."

He was young, couldn't have been a detective long, and Kay served him tea. Franklin was courteous, but a little awkward with small talk. By the time he got to the point, Kay was feeling calm and lightly amused.

"Do you know a man named Arthur Ghanbarian?"

"A long time ago, yeah. He called himself Artie Groove. I wrote songs for him."

"When was the last time you saw Mr. Ghanbarian?"

"Not since I stopped working for him—1977, '78. Around there."

"Have you had any contact with him at all: in person, telephone, letters?"

"No, nothing. What is this about?"

"Mr. Ghanbarian was found beaten to death in his apartment on Wednesday evening. Before he died he wrote your name."

"What does that mean? He wrote my name?"

"On the floor. He wrote what appears to be your name. Do you have any idea why he'd do that? Anything at all. Like were you ever romantically involved with Mr. Ghanbarian?"

"No. I most certainly was not." What the hell kind of question was that?

"Ma'am, I'm just ascertaining the facts."

9

"So every woman who worked with Artie would naturally go to bed with him, right?"

"Where were you Tuesday morning and afternoon?"

Kay was genuinely mad—asking if she'd slept with Artie then going right for the kill—*where were you Tuesday?* Fuck this pig. Franklin left soon afterward, Kay finished both cups of tea, and Emily finally came out to the kitchen.

"Nan Kay? That guy—Artie Groove?"

"You were listening?"

"He's the one who wrote that button song I was telling you about. You know—there's a button . . . on my booty? You knew that guy?"

"Emily, I wrote that song. I sang that song."

The look on the girl's face—mouth hanging open, struggling to figure out if this was an elaborate put on.

"It's my voice. My song. I wrote the arrangement. I made sure the horns played it punchy and the bassline was crisp. It's my God damned song."

"And that guy stole it from you?"

"That's what he did."

Emily had one more question to ask, but it just wouldn't come to her lips.

*

The next day a music blogger called. Some of the story had leaked. Kay told the young man that she'd written *Button* and sang it on the record. And, no, she hadn't seen Artie in forty years.

With more to go on, the story grew:

Sleaze got what he deserved, stealing from a lady.

Old bat probably killed him herself. That's why he was writing her name. Kapow.

Right8 should tour with her. Like how some rappers have a midget and dumb shit like that in the show. He should bring that lady up on stage and press down on her floppy old ass. ROFL.

A few serious music heads dug up some more of the old GrooveArt sides. It was obvious that Lana Groove was not the lead singer on *Button*. Then

10

someone found an outtake from an unreleased song called *Liquefaction*, where Artie Groove could be heard saying, "All right, Kay, let's try that again." There was a consensus growing among those who cared that Kay Olonkowski was the voice they'd been hearing all summer.

A reporter from *The Post* came to the house with a photographer and did an extended interview. For the picture they asked her to stick out her backside and point to it, but she declined. Instead they got Kay and her adoring granddaughter sitting out on the front steps: *Queens Grannie Says Button Belongs to her Booty.*

The next day a representative of Right8 called.

"We'd like to explore the possibility of you being a part of the show at the Barclays Center. We're interested in how much you are able to sing."

Kay still practiced every day, kept the cords limber. Like an eighty-year-old Marine Corps vet who did the calisthenics he learned in basic. Scales, arpeggios, breathing drills. Then she sang the old songs as she walked to work or strolled the boardwalk by the beach.

"I am able to sing," she said.

They sent a car all the way out to Far Rockaway and brought her to a studio where a young lawyer—a smart girl with no sense of rhythm—laid the contract on her.

"We are so thrilled you could make it. We really respect you as a musician, a creative personality. What we need from you now is for you to sign this. It will establish once and for all that you were the original vocalist on *Button*. We'll correct the back catalog to reflect this. It also confirms that you won't claim composition rights for this or any other song from the old GrooveArt label. Then we can discuss having you join Right8 for some live music."

"What if I don't sign?"

"Why wouldn't you sign?"

"I wrote the song, and I never got a dime for it."

"Kay, I don't think you understand what's happening here. We are trying to shine a light on your

11

talent and your voice. We don't have to do that. If you'd like, we'll provide you with transportation back to your home."

Just like always. You sang the songs, someone else paid for the drinks, the rides, the food. The best you could hope for was a few dollars at the end of the night. It wasn't right, but it was how it had always worked.

The only musician in the studio was a man at a keyboard, Marcel—about thirty-five, laid back, an ally. The first time through the chorus Kay came in a little late, but the second time she really found it, and as they took it out, she played around with the phrasing, sliding up into notes and hitting *Press it down* with sharp staccato barks. When they were done, Marcel let out one low laugh.

"If y'all don't want her, I'm taking her home with me."

As Kay signed the agreement—industry standard for backup vocals—she had the familiar feeling that she was getting steamrolled by the suits.

"So Right8 has been delayed this morning," the lawyer said, "but he really wants to get to know you. If you can wait just a little bit longer, we should have him here very shortly."

She left the musicians alone together.

"I looked back through the catalog," Marcel said. "There's some great stuff there. And you sing lead on all of it: *Groovedale Academy, Disco Gravy*. That's you, I could tell."

"I wrote both of those, too. Sometimes we'd just say stupid shit—*Funky Llama, Dancefloor Stroking*—it would become a song."

"You guys were high the whole time, right?"

"Yeah, I guess. A lot of real pricks in the business, but I can't say it wasn't fun."

With nothing else to do, they tried some of Kay's originals, then a few funk classics, a hymn. Another man peeked through the glass, curious, and Marcel waved him into the room mid-song. The man went right to the drum kit. It was so nice—just being with

12

players, finding it. In the middle of an old Stevie Wonder song, the lawyer returned.

"Can you come out here, Kay?" she said over the speakers from outside the room. The musicians looked up, annoyed to be interrupted when it was good. Marcel cut Kay's mike and spoke quietly.

"Whatever it is, you don't have to take their shit, man."

She kissed him on the mouth then left the studio and followed the lawyer into her office.

"Thank you for your time. We won't be able to use you at the show." The lawyer handed her an envelope. "This is what you would have gotten if the show had run past midnight. It's more than fair. We wish you all the best."

The lawyer stood and ushered her out of the room, toward the elevators where Kay spotted Right8, joking around with a few interns near the reception desk.

"This is the lady, right?" he said. "Ms. Olonkowski, so good to meet you. They told me you were dead, you know? A dead woman named Lana Groove. But look at you—very much among the living."

"I'm sorry, Dwayne. She won't be able to perform tonight," the lawyer said.

"She looks fine. I know she can sing." He looked right at Kay. "You can sing tonight, can't you?"

"I can sing anytime."

The lawyer tried to brush it off, but Right8 persisted. As a performer he was goofy, girl-crazy, perpetually stoned. In real life with a problem to solve, he was sharp and stubborn. The lawyer led them all back to her office.

"I've got a guy I know in the NYPD," she said. "They want to talk to Ms. Olonkowski about the death of Arthur Ghanbarian."

"They already did that," Kay said.

"New developments." The lawyer looked only at Right8 while she spoke. "If she clears all this up, maybe we can talk about doing something down the road. For right now, she needs to leave the studio."

13

"You got that backwards. We put her on stage tonight. And if they take her off in handcuffs, we bail her out and put her up tomorrow in an orange jumpsuit."

"This is a bad idea."

"No, this is an eight-million-dollar idea. She looks like every white girl's grandma, sings like she just made out with Luther Vandross, and if you steal from her, she'll put a metal pipe to your head. She's going on stage." Right8 turned to Kay. "You want to sing, right?"

"I also need to get paid."

"How much?"

"Half a million dollars."

Right8 laughed lightly.

"You know who gets 500K for one night? Beyoncé, Streisand, Kanye, Tony Blair. What do you say to thirty thousand? And if you get arrested, we handle bail."

"I don't know where you think this money is coming from," the lawyer said.

"I'll go out of pocket. But I really suggest you get me reimbursed for doing what it takes to promote the music."

Over the lawyer's objections, they walked out of the studio together—just Kay and Right8.

"And you really killed that guy?" Brain was coming out, right?" he asked her on 7ᵗʰ Avenue. "Hey, I get it— you ice a dude, you don't admit nothing to no one. Say, you got your account and routing number on you?"

The bank manager was a younger guy, a fan, a little giddy to be helping out. He put the transfer through while they waited.

"Just one more keystroke and we're all set," he said. "Would you like me to—*Press it down*?"

Right8 walked Kay to a big midtown hotel and got her a room under the name Dwayne Reid.

"We'll figure out rehearsal, wardrobe, all that—later tonight. You just relax for now. Order food, watch a movie. It's all on account—no worries. And don't tell anyone where you are."

14

It was the nicest hotel she'd been to since back in the days of industry parties at the Gramercy and the St. Regis. Yeah, she'd done her share of hard drugs, sang from midnight rooftops high above the stinking city, talked to paranoid geniuses about *where the music was headed*, used a portable skillet to help Lionel Ritchie make a western omelet. She'd been accepted on the inside because of her talent. But memories can take a lot out of you. She put soap in her purse and then fell asleep on top of the sheets. When she woke up, she decided to go out for a walk—just to the park and back. But she was picked up by police outside the hotel. She called Right8 from a payphone inside the station.

"Yeah, we can probably hold off doing *Button* until 11 if we have to. So we need to get you out by 10:30 or so—probably just have you sing the chorus live at the encore."

Kay heard the lawyer in the background—impatient, scolding.

"I will help you as much as I can," Right8 said. "That's a promise."

Maybe it was a promise, but it wasn't a strong promise. Right8 sounded less fired up, less ready to act decisively. Maybe the lawyer was wearing him down. Maybe a fifty thousand dollar investment didn't mean much to him. Maybe he'd already canceled the transfer.

The cops left her in an interview room for an hour with nothing to do. She assumed she was being recorded—audio and video. Finally a middle-aged, female detective entered the room.

"Will I be out this evening?" Kay asked.

The cop didn't quite stifle a laugh.

"We have you on the surveillance camera of a bank around the corner from Ghanbarian's place—holding a golf club. We have that club in evidence. We have prints from the club. And now we have your prints. You think it's going to be a match?"

"I never gave you my prints."

15

"You touched a lot of things. Ms. Olonkowski, it's over. We'll get witnesses, we'll find your DNA in his apartment, on the club. You can't beat the charge, but if you start working with me now, I'll see what I can do for you. Believe me—I get that Ghanbarian really screwed you over. From what I've heard he seemed like a real dick. Maybe he said something to set you off? Just write out a statement. Write what happened as best as you can remember. This is your chance to tell the story on your own terms."

Kay didn't pick up the pen, and she didn't say another word to the detective. The cop checked her phone a number of times—waiting for the fingerprint report? Finally she left the room without explanation. Kay was still there at nine, ten, and eleven o'clock. No lawyer was coming to help. They would charge her, and no one would bail her out. It didn't seem likely that she'd ever be free again. She stood in the corner of the room, out of range of the camera, but as close as she could get to what she assumed was the microphone.

She'd never been satisfied with the lyrics, but once you got in the studio, Artie moved things along fast— *get it down, get it done.* There was never enough time.

She began to sing:

There's a button. So get behind it. There's a button. Just get in line.

There's a button. If you can find it. There's a button. So take your time.

***

© 2017 Preston Lang

16

The Kid in Love

by Charles Roland

The Kid was 32 years old. He figured he was at least ten years too old for anyone to be calling him "Kid." But they called him that anyway, and money was money, so he didn't make a thing about it.

"How's The Kid looking?"

"You got a fight coming up for The Kid?"

"How you feel, Kid?"

"Looking good in there, Kid."

"Thanks," he'd say, and that was that.

The Kid tried to keep his shit low key.

*

Prison wasn't like The Kid thought it was going to be. It was way worse at Rikers Island, where he'd spent the six weeks or so before he took a plea deal and went upstate. Rikers was where you went before your trial if you couldn't make bail, and it was a fucking zoo. Even the guards were in gangs. Stabbings, beatings, all that stuff.

Part of the reason The Kid took the deal was to get out of Rikers. The other part was that he was guilty. They said it was armed robbery, but it was really more like a fight that took a turn. The Kid's buddy had had some run-in with a guy at a bodega over a girl, the guy turned out to be the owner's cousin, there was a baseball bat, the owner got involved. The Kid was there, didn't stop it, maybe threw a punch or two in the heat of things. The owner ended up in a coma, so there was that.

The Kid always figured it was the kind of dumb shit you do when you're 23 and single and barely employed. But it was *his* dumb shit, so he took the deal, did the five-year minimum, and came out the other end. His buddy went to trial and got twenty, so The Kid figured he did okay.

18

Could have been a lot worse, he thought.

*

Prison was where he picked up the boxing.

He had friends who'd been locked up, and from the stories they told, he figured it would be a nightmare. But it really wasn't that bad. Mostly there was a lot of structure, which he'd never had and found he liked, and a lot of time, which was the bitch of it.

The boxing was a way to take the structure and spread it over the time.

One of the guards coached the program, and a couple of the inmates helped out. The Kid didn't know at first if he'd take to it, but he was always decent with his hands—this was part of what got him into trouble in the first place—and he didn't want to just sit around for half of every day watching TV or whatever. So he started with the boxing, and right away he was pretty good. Over time he got better.

When he was close to getting out, the guard-coach—he was a good guy—pulled The Kid aside and said: *You have to get a job. They'll help you with that, don't worry. But you should keep going with the boxing. You're good—you know that—and the structure is good for you. You know that, too, right?*

The Kid knew it. The day he cashed his first paycheck on the outside, he walked into a boxing gym and paid the fifteen bucks for a locker, changed, and started working on the bags. Right away people noticed: *This guy knows what he's doing.* Within a couple of weeks he had a trainer, a Cuban guy called—no joke—Cuba. Cuba worked with half a dozen fighters in the evenings, wrapping hands and shouting instructions and making sure sparring sessions didn't get out of hand. The Kid liked Cuba. He was staying away from the old neighborhood and his crowd from before, so Cuba was his first real friend on the outside.

It was Cuba who introduced him to Pete Phelan. The first time The Kid met Pete, Cuba told him: "Pete's the kind of guy, you pay attention when he talks to you."

19

Pete was a big guy, somewhere in his late fifties or sixties, with thick, wavy gray hair and one of those broad, smiling faces that says: *This guy's got about a million kids and grandkids and nieces and nephews and they all love him like crazy*. His voice came from somewhere deep in his chest, so that you could hear every word he said across the room.

The Kid learned later that Pete had a construction and masonry business that was going gangbusters, and he liked to manage fighters because he'd watched the fights with his dad when he was young, and being around boxing made him feel like the old man was still around.

There was also talk that Pete knew lots of people and could make things happen—sometimes bad things, if he needed to—but people always talk, and The Kid figured it wasn't his business, anyway. So Cuba brought The Kid to see Pete, and he said: "This is the kid I been telling you about."

Pete smiled, shook his hand, looked him up and down.

"So," he said. "Cuba says you're a hell of a fighter. Says you've been to jail, too." He paused. "You straight now?"

The Kid nodded.

"You want to fight professional?"

The Kid nodded again.

Pete looked him over, took his time. Finally, he asked: "You Polish?"

"Russian," The Kid said.

"Uh huh," said Pete. "You Jewish?"

The Kid nodded, and also shrugged. His mom had always told him they were Russian, and then added "Jewish" as a kind of afterthought; she spoke Russian at home and in the neighborhood and was born somewhere in Ukraine, back in Soviet times. She threw him out of the house when he was a teenager, and he hadn't seen her in over a decade. His father was dead.

"Okay," said Pete. "Jewish fighter. That's good."

They shook hands again, and then Cuba shooed The Kid away so he could talk to Pete alone. A week later, Cuba came into the gym with a box. "From Pete," he said, and handed it to The Kid.

Inside the box was a pair of blue-and-white boxing trunks with Stars of David on the legs and "Hebrew Warrior" stitched across the top.

The Kid shrugged. *Why not?*

He had his first professional fight a month later. He knocked the other guy out in ninety seconds.

*

The Girl was 28 years old, and some of them had been tough ones. She knew it rattled The Kid a little when the guys at the fights asked about her, ran their eyes up and down her like they wanted her to know they were looking, but he didn't talk about it and she didn't bring it up.

"Who's The Girl?"

"What's with The Girl?"

"Where'd you find The Girl?"

The Kid would just say, "I got lucky." Then he'd put himself in between The Girl and whoever was asking, like: *You talk to me, not to her.*

Some girls might have thought The Kid was overprotective, possessive. Might have felt like his *back off* act cramped their style. Some girls might have shrugged The Kid off like a heavy coat in the summertime and went and played the field a little.

The Girl didn't do that, and she didn't want to, either. She liked that he was protective.Nobody every thought she was worth protecting before.

*

She'd talked to The Kid that first time because he didn't know what a smart phone was.

She was with a customer, and when The Kid walked into the store she didn't even look up. Javier caught him as he walked in: "You looking for a new phone?"

The two men talked. She finished with her customer. Javier looked her way and shook his head, like: *I can't deal with this guy.*

21

She put on her work smile and came over. "Can I help you, sir?" Javier walked away. The Kid was holding a phone sideways with both hands, like he didn't know what to make of it.

"I need a phone," The Kid said, frowning at the device in his hands.

He was cute. Tall, great shape. When he looked up she saw that he had nice eyes. Deep, soft, kind. She smiled for real this time.

"What's wrong with that one?"

He looked back down at his hands.

"This is, like, a computer." He put the device down, and mimed opening up a phone, holding it to his ear.

"I need, like, a phone."

His earnest confusion kept the smile on her face.

"They don't make those anymore," she said. "Phones look like this now."

"Oh," he said. Then he paused. "I've been away for a while."

He looked up at her again, and it was the look in his eyes this time that did it. It might have said other things to other people, but to her it said: *I can't do this without you.*

She set him up with the cheapest plan on the cheapest phone. They talked. He was sweet, a little shy. He had a great smile. Javier took care of three customers in a row.

When The Kid left with his new phone, hers was the first number in it.

At the time, The Kid was 4-0, all by knockout. The first time they hung out, he told her about the boxing. Told her about the day job delivering boxes of groceries to rich people in Manhattan. He smiled, told her about how he'd cut the tape on the boxes, snap a banana or two off a bunch, tape the box back up. "That's how I get my breakfast," he said.

He was smiling, but she could tell he was unsure of how she'd take it, testing the waters a little. Trying to make a joke of it—funny story—but really saying: *I don't have much. I have to cut corners. I struggle to get by.*

22

She smiled back, touched his arm and let her fingers rest for a second. *It's okay. We all have to get by*.

The next one was bigger. He was so nervous, he wouldn't even look her in the face. But he knew he had to talk about it. He could just say he was away for a while, and that would be that?

When he said *prison*, she wasn't scared, or even surprised. He had those soft eyes, shy ways, but she could tell he was hard, too, if it came to it. When he said it she got close to him, took his hand, leaned in. *It's okay. Everybody's got their shit. Me too, god knows*.

In truth, it probably made her like him even better when he told her. The way he said it: tentative, a little confused, like with the phone. It made her feel like he needed her. She'd always had a thing about taking care of people. *Not like that's worked out so great*, she thought.

Later that night, when they touched each other for real, he was shy again, nervous. Trying so hard to be gentle, so conscious of how small she was, how soft. It was like he was afraid he might break her.

"It's been a while," he said. That shy smile, hopeful, scared.

She calmed him, touched him, made him feel good, helped him make her feel good.

When he started to relax, she knew that she'd made him feel safe, and she was happy.

Two weeks later, he met her daughters. Their dad wasn't in the picture. Most days her mom helped out, picked them up from school, made dinner. Kids are great with shy people because they don't judge. They didn't give The Kid any time to be nervous, and the way he smiled and laughed and played made him look like a kid himself.

Shit, she thought. It was happening really fast. They spent two, three nights a week together, talked every day. He didn't say much; she didn't mind. She started going to the fights with him, cheering him on, watching him win. She met Cuba, she met Pete, she

23

met the guys in Pete's circle who'd watch the fights, smoke cigars, hit on ring card girls. They paid attention to her, and she knew that they'd want to do more, but The Kid used his big body and his quiet voice, made sure they knew how things were. Pete was a good guy. When The Kid was in the dressing room, he kept his friends in line.

If someone had asked her how she felt, she'd have said: *Safe*.
I feel safe.

*

The Kid lost a couple of decisions—slick fighters gave him trouble—but mostly he won.
He told her after one fight that he didn't really like hitting guys. He liked the discipline, and the structure—the money didn't hurt, either—but he didn't want to hurt people, didn't like it.
He needed her to hear it, needed her to tell him it was okay. She smiled, touched him, made him know that it was okay, that he was okay.

She made him know that he was safe.

*

The Nephew was an asshole, because of course he was.

Nice clothes, nice watch, nice car. Plum job working for his uncle. Pete indulged The Nephew, because he was like that. Shook his head, told anyone who'd listen: *He'll outgrow it. I was a prick at his age, too*.

Everyone called The Kid "Kid," but it bugged him when the nephew said it. It was that little smirk, like: *This guy's ten years older than me, but I call him "Kid" because I can*. Like he could just as well tell The Kid: *Go pick up my dry cleaning, get me a sandwich*, and it would happen, because he was Pete's prick nephew and he was the king of the world.

The first time The Nephew looked at The Girl, The Kid got this feeling in his stomach.

Usually when guys at the fights asked The Kid about The Girl, The Kid backed them off, no trouble.

24

But The Nephew didn't say shit to The Kid. He stepped around The Kid and went right up to The Girl. "Where'd he find you?" he said. Underneath it: *What are you doing with this jerk?*

The Girl looked up at The Kid. The Kid stepped to the side, put himself between The Girl and The Nephew.

"Got lucky," he said.

"No fucking kidding," said The Nephew. He stepped to the side, got next to The Girl again.

"You like to go out, you like to party?"

Pete heard it, put his hand on The Nephew's shoulder, tossed his head, like: *Talk to me over there.*

The Nephew looked right at The Girl, like The Kid wasn't even there.

"See you around," he said.

*

The Nephew made his move two fights later, while The Kid was in the dressing room.

Pete was talking with his friends. The girl was sitting alone. The Nephew sat down next to her. Moved closer so their legs were touching.

"So what's with you and The Kid?" He asked, sneering a little when he said *The Kid*, making sure she knew he thought it was ridiculous.

She looked for Pete. He wasn't around. Her heartbeat picked up; she was scared, a little.

She put her best *fuck off* look on her face.

"Why don't you go find your uncle?" She said. What she meant was: *Get the fuck out of here.*

The Nephew smirked.

"He's around," he said.

He put his hand on her leg.

She got up, pulled away.

"Don't fucking touch me."

She fast-walked out of the row of seats. His laughter followed her.

The ladies room was down a hall and up a short flight of stairs. She put her palms down on the counter and looked in the mirror. Her heart was still going. *Fuck*, she thought.

25

The door opened, and The Nephew stepped in behind her. He was smiling. She took a step back, trying to keep some distance between them.

"What are you doing?" She asked.

"Relax," he said. He put his palms up, like: *no problem.*

"Get away from me," she said. "Get out of here." She stepped back again. He stepped forward.

"I'm warning you, don't fucking touch me."

The Nephew stepped forward again. The Girl's back touched the wall.

"You think your boyfriend's pretty fucking tough, huh?" He said. "Watch out, everybody, it's *The Kid.*" He threw his hands up, made a mock-scared face. "Ooooh, look out."

Her hands were curled into fists. Her nails dug into the insides of her palms. Her back was pressed against the wall.

"I could make him lose," he said. "You know that?"

"Fuck you," she said.

"I could," he said. "I could tell my uncle, 'make The Kid lose,' and he would."

She said nothing. Her eyes burned. She hated him.

"Or, why not, I could have him clipped. You know about my uncle. He's got friends. I've got friends. I could say, '*The Kid threatened me, he pulled a knife on me, I was so scared.*'" He paused. "Fuck it. I wouldn't even need a reason."

"Fuck you," she said again. "You're full of shit. Pete wouldn't do that."

"Sure he would," he said. "Pete likes The Kid. Pete *loves* The Kid. But I'm family. Family comes first, you know?"

He stepped forward so that they were almost touching. He raised his hand to her face; she slapped it away.

"You think I haven't done it before?" He said, speaking softly now, staring into her eyes. "You think I haven't passed the word, someone disappears? Guys'll do it just for a favor, to help out Pete's nephew, get in the big man's good books. Pete won't know until it's done. He'll be mad, sure, but what's he gonna do? I'm family."

She dropped her eyes to the floor. She tried to hold it together, but the tears came.

He smiled.

"You tell me which one you want. Make him lose? Make him disappear? Shit, maybe both."
He raised his hand again. This time she didn't move. He touched her face. He took her shoulder and guided her into a stall, pushed her down so she was sitting. "You want to help your boyfriend out? The Kid, champion of the world, living and breathing? Here you go."

He unzipped, took it out.
Her tears were coming strong now.
She thought: *He always protects me.*
He can't protect me now.
I have to protect him.

*

The Kid won the fight. Knockout, fourth round. The Girl sat through it in a daze. It was like she was outside herself, looking down, watching herself watching The Kid.

After he'd finished, The Nephew had wiped himself with toilet paper, tossed the wad at her, zipped up. Smirk on his face.

"See you around," he said.

She cried, cleaned up, cried again, cleaned up again. Then she came back down to her seat.

After The Kid's fight, she went back to the dressing room. Cuba had already cut the tape off The Kid's hands and went to talk to Pete. Most of the other fighters on the card had already changed and gone home or come out to watch the next fight. The Kid and The Girl were alone.

He already knew that something was wrong.

"Tell me," he said.

She looked at the floor.

"Tell me," he said.

She started to cry. She wouldn't look at him. He put one arm around her shoulders, the other on her leg. He pulled her into him. His arms were so strong.

"Tell me," he said.

She told him.

*

The Kid didn't scream, didn't punch the wall, didn't get up and go looking for The Nephew.
He sat still and listened, kept his arms around her, and when she lifted her head she saw that he was crying.

"I'm sorry," he said. "I'm sorry."

They held each other and cried together, and then they got up, rinsed their faces, cleaned up. Cuba came in, grabbed his bag, said, "Take a day tomorrow, see you Monday," and took off. Pete came in, said, "Looking good, my friend," kissed The Girl on the cheek, and took off.

The Girl felt numb. The Kid was very still.

The Nephew came in.

He saw The Kid and stopped, just for a second, then kept coming. His eyes travelled to The Girl, held there for a second, then went back to The Kid. Then he smirked.

"She told you, huh?"

He held his hands up, like: *What can you do?*

"Hey, she came on to me, okay? What can I say? I'm a man, right?"

He never saw the first punch coming.

His nose exploded, and then he dropped to his knees. The Kid moved over him and punched down. The Nephew went down on his back. The Kid straddled his chest and kept hitting him.

The Girl told him to stop. She put her hands on his shoulders. He kept going. She cried, tried to pull him off. He kept going, staring down at where The Nephew used to have a face, punching slow, steady, over and over again.

The Girl didn't know how long it lasted. She turned away, put her head in her hands, tried not to hear the wet *thump*s.

*

28

The Kid was covered in blood. There was blood all over.

The Girl was curled up in a corner. She was crying. She was touching his leg.

Pete came in. He stopped. He stared. His mouth went: *Oh, shit.*

*

The same guard still ran the boxing program. He was a good guy. The Kid helped out.

The Girl visited. She brought her daughters. Once she brought her mom.

Months went by, then a year. The Girl visited less. She stopped bringing her daughters.

The Kid called. She answered less and less. He talked to her voicemail. He didn't know what to say.

He got the letter.

Can't do this anymore.

I've met someone.

I'm sorry.

I love you.

I'm sorry.

The Kid closed his eyes, opened them. Held the letter. Closed his eyes. Folded the letter back up, put it in the envelope, put the envelope on the little shelf with his books and things.

He got up, left his cell, walked down the tier toward the gym.

I love you, too.

***

29

Family Secrets

by Eric Beetner

"Daddy?" I asked. "Is that blood?"

Mom waved a hand at me, shooing me out of the bathroom as she pulled the door half closed. I could still see Dad propping himself up on one hand while the rest of him sprawled out on the tile floor. His free hand stayed pressed hard into the deep red stain on his shirt, down near his hip.

"Run and get me some towels," Mom said. "In the hall closet. The small ones, hand towels, you know what kind I mean?" She made small squares in the air with her hands to illustrate exactly what she wanted. Her palms were smeared in red.

"Yes, Momma," I said.

"Then go on and get 'em, boy." She turned her back on me and went through the door to tend to Daddy again.

Walking to the closet I tried to process what I'd seen in the five minutes, less probably, since my parents came home. I was all of thirteen that day. But what a day it turned out to be.

I opened the linen closet door and stood on tiptoes to retrieve the right sized towels. I heard Dad grunt through the walls. I'd never seen my Dad in pain before. Not that I could recall.

I piled five small hand towels in the crook of my arm and walked back to the bathroom as Dad let out another low growl. He sounded mean, like he was choking on anger.

I knocked lightly at the door. For a moment I thought Mom didn't hear me, then she jerked the door open and held out a bloody hand for the towels. Her other hand held a pair of tweezers and I noticed a tiny lump of metal swimming in a pool of blood next to the sink. If the TV shows were accurate, it looked like a bullet slug.

31

"Momma?" I let the questions go unasked. Too many to sort out in my young brain.

"I don't have time right now, baby." Mom bent her knees to get closer to my level and rubbed her tweezer hand against my shoulder, smudging it with blood. "Daddy's gonna be okay. You might run downstairs and get him a beer from the fridge. Would you do that darlin'?"

I nodded and stole glances past her to Dad who had moved all the way down to the floor. His one hand still pressed hard on his abdomen, his other clenched in a tight, pulsing fist. I walked down the steps, careful to avoid stepping in any of the drips of blood Dad trailed behind him when they came in. I didn't buy the fake sincerity in Mom's voice when she told me Dad would be okay. But beyond wondering if my father would live or die, I tried to figure out how in the world he ever came to be shot.

I look a longneck bottle from the fridge, rooted through the third drawer from the sink for an opener. I found it and popped the cap off, then stole a sip for myself. I figured I was due for a little liquid courage as much as anyone in the house.

When I reached the foot of the steps on my way back upstairs, the doorbell rang. I jumped, jerking my shoulders up high and letting the beer slip from my fingers and fall to the floor where it banged off the hardwood and fell over on its side, gushing beer onto the living room rug.

I turned and saw the shape of a large man through the frosted glass of the front door. He pounded three times. "Police! Open up."

I turned and sprinted up the steps.

When I reached the bathroom door, Mom was already out in the hall. "I heard," she said.

I stood in front of her like a fish on dry land, my mouth gaping open and shut, mute and short of breath.

"Here's what I want you to do," Mom said. "Go down there and open the door, but don't let him in. No matter what, you hear me? You do *not* let him in. If he

32

tries to come inside, and he will, you ask him if he has a warrant." She stared me deep in my eyes in a way she hadn't since she told me our dog, King, had died. "You ask him that, okay?" I nodded. "You tell him your Dad and I are not here and you don't know when we'll be back. You got that? Say that and nothing else. Can you do this for me?"

I nodded again. "A warrant," I said.

"That's my boy." She turned away from me as the policeman hammered on the door again.

I padded fast down the steps. I opened the door only as wide as my body, and stuffed myself in the opening. The cop was tall. I'd always been short so adults usually seemed tall to me, but this guy was extra-large. My eye immediately went to the gun on his belt, jutting out from his side. A big, unnatural growth.

"I need to see your Mom and Dad, son."

"They ain't here."

He eyeballed me. "They're not?"

"No, sir."

"How long have they been gone?"

Mom didn't coach me on that one. "All day, sir. Won't be back until later."

"And you're here all by yourself? No babysitter or anything?" He'd stopped looking at me and peered inside the house through the small opening I gave him.

"No, sir. Just me. I got my own key for when they're at work and stuff." I pointed past him to the small potted flower on the porch. He followed the tip of my finger and stepped over to the pot, lifted it, and removed the key underneath.

"You shouldn't keep a key right there, son." He flipped the key once in his hand and held it out to me. "First place a burglar is gonna look."

I took the key and stuffed it in my pocket. "Okay. I'll tell my Mom and Dad."

"You tell them I stopped by too." He tried to get one more look over my head. "Maybe I'd better come in and look around."

33

"You got a warrant?" I asked. At the time, I barely knew what a warrant even meant. But I was a good boy and did as my Momma told me.

The cop gave me suspicious look. I noticed for the first time two more cops in the yard, each with a hand on the butts of their guns.

"Son, I don't need a warrant if I got a reasonable suspicion of illegal activity." He rested the heel of his own hand on his gun. "Is someone in there with you?"

"No, sir. I told you."

"We're here to help, boy. If someone is keeping you against your will . . ."

I felt a hand on my shoulder and I nearly jumped out of my skin. Mom breezed past me, filling up my space in the door.

"Officer, what's the trouble?" She knew I was losing it. She had to step in.

"Ma'am is this your son?"

"Yes."

"He told us you weren't home."

"I just got back. Came in through the back door. What's the trouble?"

"Ma'am, I need to speak to your husband."

"He's not here. What's the matter?" Mom got a convincing sound of panic in her voice.

"Do you know where he is, ma'am?"

"At work I suspect. Why won't you tell me what's wrong?"

"Ma'am, I need you to come with me." The officer held out a hand and Mom shied away from it in a way I'd never seen from her. She was full of surprises that day. I looked at her hands, expecting to see blood, but they were clean with little drops of water in the thin hairs on the backs of her hands. The air around her smelled like soap.

"Yes, of course. Will you tell me what's going on when we get to the station?"

"Yes, ma'am."

Mom bent down to speak to me. "You'll be all right, dear. I'll be home in time for dinner. If your father

34

comes home, tell him where I am and that the police wish to speak with him."

Her words flew through me without meaning. I read her eyes. They pleaded with me to help Dad. To not give up her secret. They told me she had to go, to lure the cops away if Dad was to have any chance at all. I understood.

"He can come too," the cop said.

"I'd rather he not have to see a police station when he's so young. Besides, he has homework to finish."

"I'll be okay," I said.

Watching her climb into the police car was like watching her drive away in the back of a hearse. As I closed the door I noticed three drops of blood in a cluster on the threshold. One look down from the cop and we would have been sunk.

I went upstairs to Dad. I eased the door open slowly. Only when the hinge creaked did Dad look up from the floor. His skin was pale and glazed with sweat.

"Your Mom?" he asked, his voice a dry creek.

"She went with the cops."

Dad coughed, swallowed something back. "In handcuffs?"

"No."

"Good, good." He pushed himself up with a stifled groan until he could lean his back against the bathtub. Over his shoulder, in the basin of the tub, I saw pink stains of blood mixed with the water used to wash it away. Down the sides of the tub ran long red veins of drying blood. Near the drain was another crumpled metal slug rimmed in darker blood and something thicker.

"You need to do me a favor, boy." Dad gave me detailed directions to a hiding place in his bedroom and a description of the box I was to find there.

I found it no problem. I brought the small wood-carved box to him. He lifted the lid, revealing a shiny pistol nestled in a molded case. Two neat rows of six silver bullets glinted in the bathroom light. I'm sure the bullets were nickel or some other metal, but to me right then, they were pure werewolf killers.

I wanted to ask about the gun, about his wounds, about what the hell was going on, but I kept my mouth shut.

The doorbell rang again. Dad jerked his head up from looking at the gun and immediately went into a coughing fit. The box slid off his lap and I picked it up and put it on the counter next to the bloody slug.

"What should I do, Daddy?"

He tried to get out the words, but he kept on coughing. A spray of blood came out and I felt tiny droplets on my face.

He never had time to answer. The door downstairs burst open, the frosted glass shattered and fell to the floor. I heard it and turned to my Dad with terror in my eyes.

"Duke?" a voice boomed from the first floor. Dad coughed more, betraying our location. Wasn't much of a hiding place anyhow.

Feet thundered up the steps like a rodeo bull got loose in the house. Two men turned into the hallway and marched toward the bathroom. Both tall, in jeans and heavy work jackets. Each had a gun in his hand. The man in front wore a goatee trimmed to a point below his chin, his partner wore a greasy baseball cap with a car parts logo.

They ignored me as they stepped into the doorway. The goateed man smiled when he saw the blood, my Dad slumped over against the bathtub.

"Guess I did wing you, huh?" He turned to his partner. "Told ya'"

I stood by wondering why Dad didn't shoot. These men obviously came to do him harm. Then I saw the gun box on the counter. I'd disarmed my Dad and he wasn't up for lunging for a gun or any other acts of heroics.

"Where's Wanda?"

I heard my Mom's first name so infrequently I didn't immediately know who he was talking about.

36

"Fuck you," Dad said. I heard my Dad curse even less frequently.

"Tough talk for a guy with half his guts on the bathroom floor."

Being small, my Dad felt the need to teach me a thing or two about fighting bullies. I'd never had cause to use any of the lessons, but Dad drilled them into me anyway. His basic premise was: fight dirty.

I stood there, not knowing a thing about what was going on, only that my Mom and Dad were in trouble and these guys were here to finish a job they started. Dad's training took over.

I lifted my right leg and planted a foot into the crotch of the guy with the goatee. He bent in on himself like a crushed soda can. His friend with the hat jumped forward and made a move to pistol whip me. I guess shooting a thirteen year-old was where he drew the line, violence-wise.

When his arm reached above his head I threw a straight jab with my left hand into his balls. He also bent in half and his gun fell from over his head, nearly striking mine.

Dad never trained me for the next part.

I picked the gun up and fired. Two shots into the guy with the hat, both chest shots up around his heart which was no feat of marksmanship since he stood all of twelve inches away from me. Then I spun and, before the first man even hit the ground, I put two bullets into the tough talker. One through his chest and one in his neck right below the point of his stupid half beard.

The man with the hat landed and his head came to a rest on top of my shoe. The man with the goatee slumped forward into the bathroom and ended up face down next to Dad's legs, spewing blood from his neck onto the already bloody bathroom tile.

The look on Dad's face was even more surprised than the time he walked in on me with an open Penthouse and a box of tissues.

I put the gun on the counter like I was setting down the toothpaste after brushing my teeth. My brain hadn't yet processed what I'd done. I slid my foot out from under the head of the man I'd killed and his hat slipped off unveiling a bald spot in a final insult to his vanity. Killed by a kid a third his age and now his hairline secret is revealed.

"Daddy?" I said.

"You did good, kid." He closed his eyes and smiled. His smile only lasted a second before another wave of pain gripped him and his face twisted. "Come here," he said.

I stepped close to him, moving my sneakers over the tangle of bodies on the floor. Trying to avoid the blood was pointless.

"You did great, kiddo." He gave another weak smile. "But listen, this isn't the end. These two guys, they're nothing. There are gonna be more." He lifted the hand away from his gut for the first time. Blood dripped off each trembling finger. "I doubt I'll make it that long anyhow. I guess I'll be lucky if I don't. These guys are pretty pissed off." He started to laugh, but it quickly became another coughing fit. He pushed down on his gut again, I thought maybe to keep everything inside.

"Daddy what . . . what happened?"

"Son, your Dad's not the guy you thought he was." He looked like he wanted to tell me everything, but the words eluded him. "I made some people mad. It sometimes happens in my job. I was trying to make some extra money. For you and Mom." He tried to sit up straighter, but the attempt failed. "It's my fault though. Don't think for a second this has anything to do with you."

We both looked down at the bodies and knew it had a lot to do with me now.

"Look, son," he said. "I'm not going to make it. And you need to get out of here."   Tears came to my eyes and threatened to fall. "I want you to do me a favor. I've seen how you were just now, I know you're my little man. Scratch that, my big man." He winced in pain. "If they send more guys. No, *when* they send more, it's not gonna be pretty. I want you to do it for

38

me. I don't want them to get me. They'll make it last. They'll do things. I'd rather you do it."

I took a step back, banged into the counter. I turned and stared at the open gun box and, next to it, the pistol I'd already used. The smell of gunfire still hung in the air, the stench of clotting blood too.

"Daddy, I can't."

"You can, son. I saw what you can do."

"But, they were gonna kill you."

"Exactly. And so will the next bunch."

"What about Mom?"

"If she comes back at all it will be with the police, and they won't make it any easier on me."

I stopped hearing what he had to say. It wouldn't process. The two assassins I'd killed hadn't sunk in yet and my own father was telling me to kill him.

"Do you hear me?" he said.

I snapped out of it and nodded a lie. He gave me directions to a stash of money outside the house. He didn't say where he got it or how much. "Enough," was all he said about it.

"Hand me that box," he said.

I gave him the gun. With two bloody hands he loaded two bullets into the cylinder, but that was all he could manage. He snapped the gun shut and let the box fall to the floor.

"You won't do it, huh?"

"Daddy . . . I can't."

"I understand," he said. He swallowed hard, his eyes gone glassy. He lifted the gun and pointed it at me. "Then get the fuck out."

"Daddy."

"You can't be here when they come back, or when the cops come. You go find that money. You get out of here and keep on going. You're a man now."

I thought about my friend Steven from school and how he wouldn't stop talking about his Bar Mitzvah and how it made *him* a man. We both laughed at the absurdity of it all. He would laugh extra hard at this. All he had to do was memorize some Hebrew, not shoot a couple guys.

39

Dad drew back the hammer on the gun. "Go on."

Right then I knew he wouldn't be alive when more men came. Or if Mom came back. He was damn near bled out by then anyway, but as soon as I got a block or two away from the house, one of those bullets was going in his brain.

There was nothing I could say. No goodbye. The day I learned my father was a criminal, the day he died in front of me, is a day I've thought of every sunrise since.

I took the gun off the counter, the one I'd used. I didn't know what else to do. I stopped in my room and threw a few things in a backpack, then left to find the money.

In a way I regret not saying anything before I left, but to this day I can't think of a thing I would have said.

Mom went to prison. Twenty-five to life. She's up for parole next year. I've never been to visit and we've never written each other.

The money lasted a long time. Ten years before I got a real job, and it put me through college. I toyed with going into law, but it seemed like what I was supposed to do rather than something I wanted. An attempt to balance the scales.

Instead I have a boring job and I like it. I've never fired that gun again. I drive a sensible car, never get too drunk and get to bed by ten. I'm an average guy with a big secret. I guess some things run in the family.

***

© 2017 Eric Beetner

DOWN & OUT

THE MAGAZINE

Vol 1
Iss 1

Featuring a NEW
Moe Prager story by
Reed Farrel Coleman

With stories by
Eric Beetner
Michael A. Black
Jen Conley
Terrence McCauley
J. Kingston Pierce
Thomas Pluck
and more!

Edited by Rick Ollerman

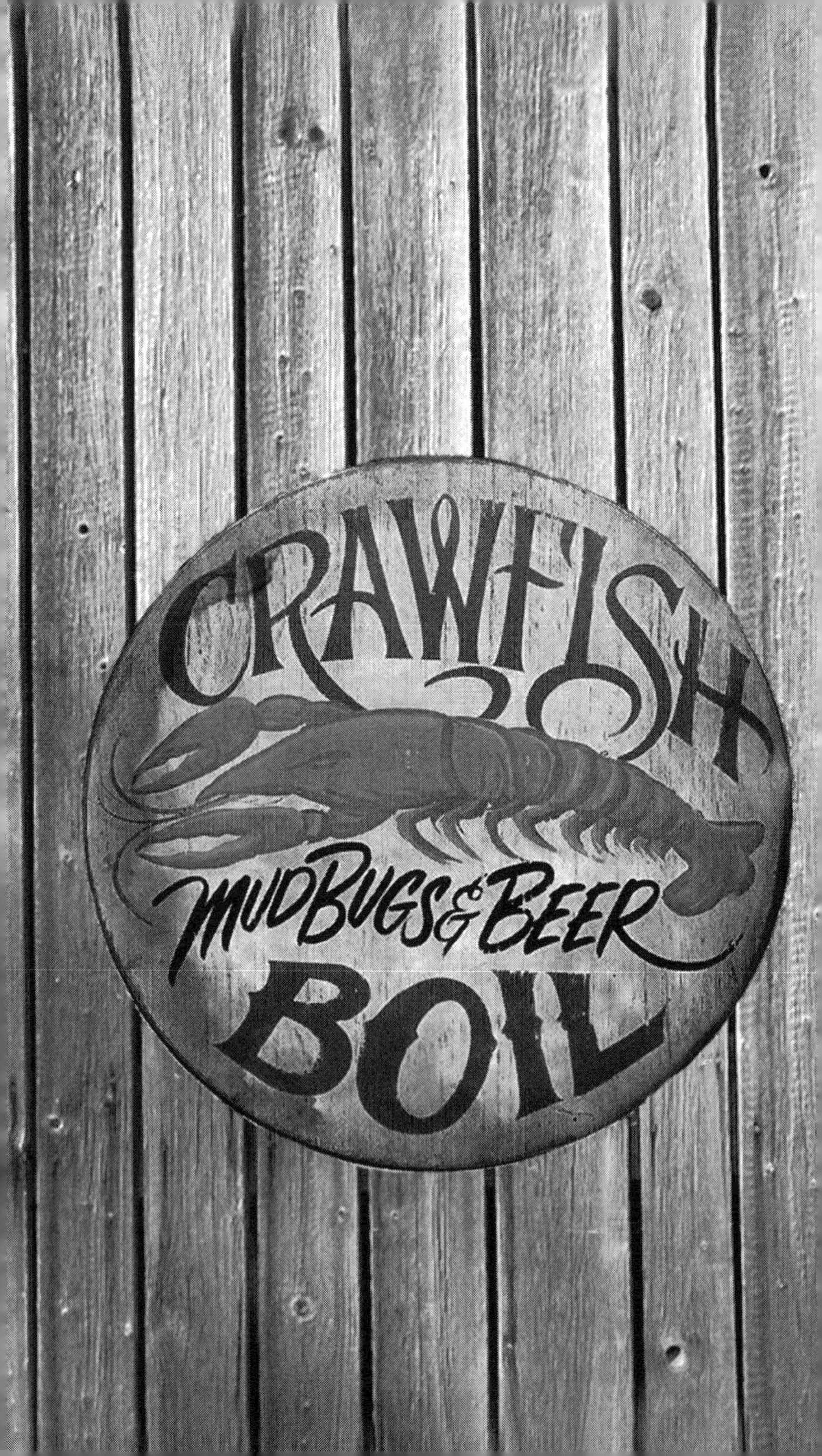
CRAWFISH
MUDBUGS & BEER
BOIL

Crawdaddy

by J.D. Graves

"Sun'll be up in a few," Deputy Jones says holding a flashlight over me. "C'mon now. These bodies ain't gonna bury themselves."

"Yessa boss," I growl and my shovel digs in. The soil's loose but I somehow knew it still would be.

I know you don't know me from Adam but I swear I ain't the murdering type. Never in a million years—I taught Sunday school for crying out loud—but each spadeful's a memory that I just wanna forget.

*

My Michelle's scared. Tears ran down her brown cheeks, across the fingers of the hand around her throat. One good squeeze and the man could snap her twig. I didn't know the man but he came with Faro, both swarthy and slick in the light of my crawfish stand. I'd only been gone—hell—I don't know how long it took to rinse the coolers, but when I got back we had visitors.

"Can you please let her go?" I hollered above the burner noise, "I'll pay whatever just—leave my daughter alone. She ain't done nothing."

Faro shook his head and the gold chain glistened underneath his neck fur. His brusque accent murdered the English language, "You had chance pay. But refuse. Blackie think I not serious. Main! I serious. I serious big time!"

I showed him my palms, "I'm serious too. Name your price."

Faro barked at me, "You fuck my father. Now I fuck you."

Suddenly I'm unsure of his exact meaning, but I got the gist and protested, "I never did no such thing."

"I count. You think I no count. I count," Faro pointed his finger at me, "Four hundred pound at seven dollar a pound is thirty-five hundred. Thirty percent is fifteen

43

hundred dollar. You no steal money no more." Then the fool whipped out a Bowie knife.

"Whoa!" I shouted not knowing what else to say. Faro's math's off, but since he's flashed a blade, I assumed he don't want no tutorial. The math genius and his friend held my Michelle between me and my Smith and Wesson. The one I kept hidden under the sink. Big good it did me then. Faro's friend tightened his grip on Michelle, her breath a ragged pump. I knew the trailer's too narrow to play hero but—I turned to the cash register and dinged it open.

"Here," I said, "take it. Take it all. Just. Let. Her. GO."

Faro glared at the paper in my hands and snorted, "That no fifteen hundred dollar."

I said, "Feel free to count—"

"You had chance," he said, "now—no chance."

I'm sure he didn't realize I blocked the only exit. He only blocked my gun and my propane burners. Which I'd told Michelle to turn off, which she hadn't. Typical teenage bullshit. The stand's hot and this situation— only made it hotter. A man's gotta know his limits and I said, "Where in the hell do you get off saying I owe you thirty? The deal I had with your daddy was ten percent."

"You rob from him three year," Faro shouted, "deal now only for thirty percent. That's ten for each year you rob."

"I don't know where the hell you're from but in this country a deal's a deal until both sides agree it ain't. You're father and I—"

"My father in hospital," He sneered, "you deal only with me Blackie."

"Well," I seethed, "I don't much like how you conduct your father's business. I'll park my crawfish stand someplace else."

Faro pointed the blade at me, "Your trailer stay. Part of your debt to me now."

"In this country you can't steal a man's—"

Faro spat on the floor, "Where I come from, man pay debt one way or another when it time for collect."

44

My blood boiled. This bastard turned and ran that knife over Michelle's thin frame, as if he sharpened a wet stone.

"Don't do that!" I yelled, "I'm warning you!"

Faro paid me no mind what-so-ever and cut away the straps of her tank top. Michelle's eyes went round, "Daddy-uh!"

I watched in horror as Faro's friend shakes her like a chicken, choking the words in her throat. Then Faro, that dumb bastard, ran his greasy hands over her goods like he's buying ripe produce—fter that everything sort've goes red.

I mean that's the only color I saw.

Like when you close your eyes outside on a sunny day.

I yelled something not worth repeating and the next thing I knew Faro slumped over, blood gushing from the dent in his skull. His limbs sizzled like bacon and then—my iron skillet dripped blood. It happened so fast. We all stared dumbfounded at the flopping man between us.

Faro's friend howled and my Michelle screamed and skidded into Faro's puddling blood. I bent to help and didn't see the—

"Daddy!" Michelle cried.

"Fetch help!" I croaked before the friend throttled my brisket. I'm too busy swinging at the bastard to notice her leave. We trampled all over Faro as he slung me every which-a-way in the galley. I swang the skillet, but the hands choking me block all good shots—I thought—of all the ways to die, this one ain't on my short list.

He drove me to the floor so hard I lose the pan. All I could do's then's flap my arms and stare up at the hate on his face. Everything dimmed except for the fireworks popping like blood vessels all around. Faro's warm blood soaked my back. My hand flopped against the sink's trap-pipe. My gun stared back at me like a nosey neighbor mockingly out of reach.

The bastard loosened his grip to slug me in the. mouth.

WHAMP!

I winced in intolerable pain as a tooth cracked.
WHAMP!

My maw filled and leaked. My skull ached as he
slug me ag—

WHAMP! WHAMP!

My arms and legs tingled with pins and needles.
The world slipped away.

All of sudden air rushed into my lungs and I rolled
in convulsive gasps on the floor. The friend had let me
go. I got to my knees woozy reaching for the—

Then cold pressure against the side of my head. I
closed my eyes tight and waited for the boom from my
Smith and Wesson. He shouted and the hammer
clicked.

Then clicked again and again and—I
remembered—

Relief burst from my lungs. I knew exactly what that
bastard thought, 'What good's keeping a gun around
unloaded.' He screamed. I rolled away and the bastard
slipped—maybe it's the blood...

I reached out to steady myself, and I'll be damned if
I didn't find the boiling pot. It burned like hell. I jerked
back and all one hundred-sixty quarts of boil splashed
off the burner. Faro's friend squealed and writhed in
the middle of this waterfall. I lifted myself away,
looking down and—Steam, full of cayenne and
jalapeño, stung my eyes. I couldn't stop crying. The
bastard bellowed in honking gurgles, glurg-gluRG-
GLURG rising like a whistle. I rubbed my eyes clear—

The horror.

Red blisters replaced the black hair on his neck,
head and arms. He lifted his head and—

I've never in my nightmares seen a face scalded
like this. His left eye was swollen and leaked white
jelly. A hive of waxy bubbles appeared where he once
had a nose. His lips, burst from the heat, spilling
torrents of blood. All of him stained orange with
delicious cajun spices. At once, I felt sorry for him. I'm
not saying it's guilt but I did pity him and what's
happened, since I'm the one who done it.

46

He screamed and shook and shook and—
screamed and scampered backwards, honking like a
frightened goose, banging into shelves, and tumbled
out the door.

The way he stumbled around he must've gone
blind. It's the only way to explain what happened next.
How could anyone have missed the speeding squad
car? The red and blue flashers drew my eyes towards
the road. Faro's friend cast a long strobing shadow
before—

If he made a sound it's lost on impact. The brakes
squealed and that bastard slumped to the other side.

The door opened and here's where I met Deputy
Jones.

The spotlight flashed me, "Don't move! Keep your
hands where I can see 'em."

The spotlight swiveled around. That's when I
noticed my Michelle. She's in the back seat, banging
on the glass. Instinctively I moved to her—

"I said freeze nigger!" He flashed me again with his
beam, "Put your hands above your head and get on
your knees or so help me—!"

My stomach dropped. Not because this guy's
calling me names—I've been called worse—it's cause
I know at once he ain't gonna be fair with me…with
us…with this—this looks bad…real bad—I wonder
how I'll explain. I don't doubt there's a gun on me so I
moved slow as a sunrise to my knees. I never took my
eyes off Michelle. She cried and cried and—

The shadows swiped across the other side and he
says, "Jesus Christ!"

The cruiser's radio sounded off. Jones answered,
"Checking a disturbance at the Stop-N-Go off Highway
Nine…"

"That place still in business," the voice asked.

"Barely," the cop said.

"Do you need any backup Deputy Jones?"

He hesitated then replied slow, "No. Situation under
control. I'll get back with you later."

The radio crackled to silence. Michelle looked at
the front seat, watching him watch her.

47

I heard footsteps, "Are you this girl's daddy?"

I nodded as she fogs the glass with her breath.

He drawled, "How old?"

I hesitated then say, "Sixteen."

"Hmmm," he drawled again, "I found her running down the highway half naked. You know anything about that?"

I squinted at the light, "Yeah I sent her for help."

"What for?"

"I—I—" Doggone it. What's wrong with me? I stammered. I sounded ludicrous, "I-I just needed help."

"Help?" He asked, "Looks to me like you still got a face—unlike your friend back yonder."

His lack of regard for my suffering irritated me, but I gathered my wits enough to spill the beans about Faro's daddy, about our arrangement, about his heart attack, about his grieving son and the attempted extortion. I started to call it attempted rape but I ain't got no proof, save for the cut straps of Michelle's shirt.

The cop's a stone while I talked. I finished my story and finally asked, "Can my daughter get out now?"

"Not yet," he said strolling over, peeking into my crawfish stand. He shined a light at what's left of Faro, "Well ain't that a disgrace."

He's white. Athletic but short. To me, it appeared he don't own a neck since his ears and shoulders are about the same. A bright red goatee anchored a heavy face—his mother must've been a junk-yard dog. He surveyed the place, thumbing his lower lip deep in personal reflection. There's something about this man, this cop, that don't sit right with me.

"Ain't you gonna call a paramedic or something?" I asked.

"Mind your Goddamn business nigger." He grunted and turned away, unzipping his pants then—pissed, right there in front of God and everyone, on my trailer's wheels. This savage ain't got the common decency to shake twice, wheeling back around, rubbing his red mouth hair again. He squated eye level with me, "Looks like you're in a heap of it now boy."

48

I didn't respond and he smiled, "I got two dead bodies, a foxy little runaway and a helluva bullshit story."

I protested, "It ain't—"

"Did I say you could talk boy?"

I cut my eyes at him and he continued, "This is how I see it: There ain't no way out of this for you unless you do everything I say and I do mean everything. If I say jump you'd better ask me how high."

I felt Michelle watching me watching him. He drawled, "Listen boy, your story got more holes than a Tijuana whorehouse."

"What you mean?"

"I think it's best for all if this goes away, don't you?"

"I don't know what you're talking about—"

"Sure you do," The cop said. "Ain't a jury in this county gonna find you innocent. Two dead bodies. A frightened girl. They gonna give you the chair."

"It was self-defense," I said, "my daughter can corrabor—"

"That may be the case," he said, "but that ain't going down on my report—ever."

"It's the truth!"

"Yeah…the truth is whatever I say it is. Who they gonna believe? Me, a peace officer or a cold blooded murderer like you?" The Deputy said this next part slow, "So my only question's what's salvation worth to you?"

"I dunno—" I said and meant it.

He looked at me long then spits, "Yeah it's stupid anyhow. Downtown we go."

"Wait a second," I said. "I didn't mean to kill 'em."

"Save it for the judge nigger, opportunity don't knock but once—"

"Now wait please," I said this before I know I'm saying anything. "What exactly are you getting at?"

He smiled and told me his plan. It's absolutely horrible and to make sure I know his zipcode he added, "I want forty percent."

I wrinkled my nose, "How do you figure?"

"You really gonna haggle with me over this?" He sneered, "You're more of a fool than I thought."

"I know we ain't trading horses," I said, "but that's a lot of scratch. It don't seem fair."

"I'm the only one in this wide world of sports that can make all this go away," Deputy Jones said. "For that privilege it'll cost you forty percent. I could go fifty, hell I could want it all but I believe it's hard enough for a man to make a living. So take it or else try your luck—"

I paused. I knew lady justice ain't blind, but I looked at Michelle and agreed to everything. It felt like I'm outside my own bended knee body, groveling to this pale lump. I could only imagine what my Michelle sees—from inside the car.

I loaded the bodies, stacking them like heavy cordwood. He hid his cruiser behind the gas station. Then the three of us squeezed into my truck's cab. The dash-clock read five after midnight. Michelle sat against my side as I steered away from one crime scene headed for another—the whole drive I kept feeling his eyes move up and down my Michelle.

"Keep your eyes on the road," He commanded when he caught me watching him watching her.

"Where we goin'?" I asked.

"Just a little out of the way spot I know," He said and Michelle pressed against me uneasy. I looked—now the lawman's looking with his hands too.

"What are you trying to—" I stammered and immediately his hand vanished from her leg. He showed me his palms and smiled, "No need to get upset Dad. Weren't no harm meant. Not a lot of wiggle room. My hands gotta go someplace."

"You'd better keep 'em to yo—"

"Or what?" He sneered.

"Or I'll," I stammered again like a fool. "I-I-I may lose the grip of the wheel and drive us into oncoming traffic—"

"Take a look around," He said, "ain't no one else out here but us. Besides, would you really risk harm to your pretty little girl here?"

I dropped my tone, "She ain't none of your concern."

"That's fair enough," He said and crossed his arms. "In a mile there'll be a dirt road. When you see it, take it."

I do on both accounts. The road's bumpy and in need of repair but solid enough. The path opened to a clearing beside the water. He told me to stop and kill the headlights. When I saw the handcuffs my volcano rumbled, "What them for?"

"Insurance," He said and turned to Michelle. "Put your hands out darling."

I scowled, "Ain't no need for that."

He looked at me cross and added, "Either she volunteers or I take 'em. Which do you prefer?"

Michelle looked to me and I said, "Neither. There ain't no need for restraints. She's a good girl, she won't do nothing."

He nodded, "And this's my assurance she won't. C'mon we don't got all night."

I started to protest but Michelle stopped me and with a resigned strangeness said, "It's okay—How long will you be gone?"

She extended both hands at Jones. The wolf took my baby and crooned, "We'll only be a minute."

He weaved the cuffs around the wheel. We left Michelle alone in the cab. He helped drag the bodies, leading me far enough away I can't see the truck no more.

"Alright," He said with a huff, "this spot's as good as any."

He handed me a shovel, standing and watching me sweat in the hole. I didn't go very deep. We pushed Faro and the man in and after they're covered, we stood wordlessly over their graves. Part of me wanted to say something, but—what the hell would that be?

The Deputy finally sighs, "If I was you, and thank god I'm not, I'd forget where we buried this here treasure."

"What's next?" I asked.

"You really gotta ask?"

51

"I-I-I"

"Save your breath you stuttering fool," He said, "you're going back to your life. The way it was before…ain't nothing happened to change that. Put my money aside in a bank bag—other than that we don't know each other."

"But…what about Michelle?"

"I thought she weren't no concern of mine?"

"She ain't but what if she says—"

He grabbed the shovel and left my question in the air. I dropped it and followed. We drove back in silence, parting at the gas station the same way.

The sun rose as we got home to our trailer. Neither of us got out. I felt I should say something but again—what the hell—Thankfully Michelle broke first, but after she did I wished otherwise. She offers me a simple question, one I'd thought I could answer, "What have you done Daddy?"

"I-I-I did what I thought I needed to—for you."

Her eyes watered and she half shouted, "Don't blame me for this Dad!" She's out and stomping into our trailer before the truck's door closes. I stew for a minute in my own choices.

I knocked on her bedroom door. I begged her to let me in. Nothing stirred. For the next several days she was a ghost. She never left her room, at least not while I was home. I'd find vague traces of her in the kitchen: dirty dishes, open cabinets, a faint whiff of her perfume. The school called and I lied saying she was sick. But then again, maybe she was—I know I am. My belly ache ain't never going away. I went sleepless for two more days. When I finally crashed out, I didn't dream. I'm up after an hour sweating and thinking I heard things outside.

Of course there ain't nothing there. There's never really anyone—I realized there's no need to beat myself up.

I went back to my happy place, my Crawfish stand. I lit the burners, dropped the mudbugs and rinsed the coolers. My customers came and went as they please which pleased me. But I don't like them asking me when the gas station's opening again.

I told them the truth, "I don't know."

When the police stop by I lied, "Yeah I ain't seen that man's boy for some time. If he ain't at the hospital with his daddy, I don't know where he run off."

They asked me more questions. I answered them and then those boys asked me the same questions, as if they'd already forgotten my answers. I started to oblige them when I caught sight of a spook walking down the highway. My breath hitched. The police turned to see me watching her watching us.

She's fixed her hair and done her make-up kinda thick. Even still she's one of the prettiest gals I ever saw. They greeted Michelle politely and asked her questions too, leading her a few yards away. A customer arrived forcing me to drop s'more bugs. The noise makes it impossible to hear. I can only read her body—stiff, unsmiling, her eyes squinting in the afternoon sun. Every now and then she glanced my way. She spoke, for what seems like forever.

I can say with all honesty, I've never been more afraid in my life. There's no telling what children are capable of these days. I wished I'd gotten to talk to her before the police. At least we could've solidified our story—Lord knows what she's said. The cops looked back at me frowning. Then nodded at Michelle and left. My baby walked around the back of the stand. I finished with my patron and go to join her.

Michelle wetted a pool of crawfish with a water hose. She faced away with her hips cocked sideways. The way she stood made her more woman than a girl. A lump jumped in my throat as I recalled the baby I once held, who's here now but not really.

I smiled, "It's good to see you again—dar"

She cut me off, "I didn't tell 'em nothing."

"Well," I said, "why would you? Nothing to tell really."

"Is that how you're getting through this Dad?" She asked still facing away. "Just like mama—"

"That ain't fair Michelle and you know it."

53

She ran the water back and forth over the scuttling life in the kiddie pool and says, "That Deputy came by the house today. Said he wanted to remind of you of the bargain."

"I ain't forgot," I said before asking, "is that all?"

"Mostly."

"Whaddaya mean mostly?"

She crimped the hose and walked it back.

"I asked you a question girl."

She twisted the spigot and all the life runs out of it, "Why'd you do it Daddy?"

I swallowed, "I dunno...tense situation I—Know that I made a mistake. I done a terrible thing but I swear to God I did it for you baby. Those guys were gonna hurt—"

"Not that Dad," she said. "Everything after. Why'd you agree to get mixed up with that...that man?"

My neck hair prickled, "Has he done something to you?"

She didn't respond. Her eyes rolled and I saw the bruises around her neck, faint fingers through the make-up. They're slowly healing. That bastard reaped what he sowed. A memory flash made me shudder and I said, "I know it's a lot to go through. More questions than answers. But Michelle if we stick together I know we can get outta this—"

"There ain't no getting out of this," she's exhausted.

"You gotta keep hope alive baby or—"

"Car pulling in Daddy." She said flatly and went back to work. I let her go, no use in arguing—because when you get down to it, work's the only thing that ever gonna make you free. If you throw yourself into it, everything else won't matter. At the end of the day we clear around a grand. I put Deputy Jones's cut aside, but he don't show.

I do the same every night for two weeks and still nothing. By this time I've finally gotten some more sleep. Michelle's gone back to school. Hell—I'm happy for her—she needed her routine. It'll help her forget. When she asked to spend the night at a friend's house I said yes with relief.

The knock comes in the middle of the night. I knew who it was before I saw his red goatee. He comes in when I opened the door—not in uniform but dressed in black from head to toe. His boots muddy.

"We got a problem," he said while I wiped the sleep from my eyes. "They's some bold talk down at the station. Seems a dog done found a human femur bone. They're searching the woods. Nowhere near our spot, but it's only a matter of time."

"You're not suggesting we dig up them bodies?" I asked more awake now, "Then do what with 'em?"

"We gonna move 'em."

I hesitated. The thought of doing it again makes me sick.

"I'm telling you, it's only a matter of time, besides—" He said, "They're beginning to suspect you."

I'm so pissed, "I thought you was gonna take care of all this!"

Deputy Jones leaned in close, "What I've done will work as long as those bodies ain't never found. Do you understand? Or do you need me to spell it out for you again?"

I nodded quietly, seeing the picture clearly and everything, and I do mean everything blurred into focus. I dressed and he said, "Now I just need two things from you: a shovel and my money."

When I followed him out I couldn't shake this awful feeling. I'm on the bottom of the kiddie pool with the other crawdads. I'm breathing and moving. But I can hear the gas burners and smell the peppers. And know it's only a matter of time before I'm put on to boil myself.

Deputy Jones flashlight casts my shadow into the hole I've dug. I stick my shovel in and there's definitely something on the other end.

"I think we've struck oil."

"Well," Deputy Jones says, "you want a cookie nigger? You best be getting 'em out now."

"Yes sir," I says. I bend over to clear the dirt by hand and I halt, "you hear that Jones?"

"I don't hear nothing—"

55

"Hush your cracker mouth and listen," I whisper.

The woods are quieter than God's answer. Then softly in the distance—barking. My heart's a continuous high hat splash.

"Damn," Deputy Jones crouches and mutters, "this ain't good."

Deputy Jones's flashlight swipes off of me towards the sound and I can't believe my luck—with his head turned away like this, he never sees it coming.

Time no longer exists. My blood freezes. My grip rattles the shovel. An invisible hand pulls me over the line and I swing it hard. There's a boney thwamp—and I swing again. Deputy Jones never makes a sound as I shove his fat ass into the hole. With the dogs barking louder I shovel dirt as fast as I—

My mind stumbles my legs through the swamp. I'm trying to find my way back. I tell myself, I did what I had to do. What any man who loves his children would—I think about Michelle as I scramble across this black earth.

I hope she remembers me and everything I ever done for her. The last thought brings another: Two wrongs don't make a right. And yet as my legs continue to run, my light bulb turns on again: two left turns will eventually take you right. I knock brush aside with both hands and stumble onto dry land. With dawn threatening I see the truck's only a few feet away. I can hear words along with the barking now. I know I'm not perfect nor do I pretend to be, but I do love her—as much as anyone can really love another.

This I hope she knows—and with time…forgives.

Every Saint's a sinner until they're dead.

***

The Rook

Ehren Baker

When Mrs. Eriksen first hired D & D Ancestry she never imagined her lineage would amount to much of anything, and in fact had suspected from the start that the shady genealogy business was little more than a scam.

But now thumbing through the dossier on Mr. Harper's desk, she was dumbfounded to learn that her ancestors were none other than Danish royalty, great kings and queens, and that her bloodline had somehow remained pure enough over the centuries that she still held a level of claim to the throne. The fantasy nearly carried Mrs. Eriksen off.

The splendid woman's eyes and mouth hung agog, pleasing Mr. Harper as he watched her from his side of the desk. The stout, ageless hustler looked like a circus bear in his poorly tailored suit. The cuffs fell comically short and when the self-important proprietor lounged, as he did presently, kicking his feet up on the desk, he looked somewhere between a pimp and a debonair fool. But he always got his money.

That was the only thought rolling through that thickset skull of his and Mr. Harper sneered a bit, biting down on his cigarette, and taking in the peace of his measly office. Sure, outside those filthy streets rang with the cacophony of traffic and emergency sirens – the shouts and clamoring of a vastly overpopulated city. But in here, Harper was a king.

With ash trailing long on his cigarette, Harper swooped forward dexterously. The chair gave a squeal and he stubbed out the smoke as Mrs. Eriksen slowly came out of her daze.

An astonished starriness hung about her pinched, goat's face. She quit flipping through the pages in the binder and settled low in her spindle back chair and gave a few girlish swivels. "Is it always like this?"

Not sensing any skepticism, but airing on the side of caution, Mr. Harper grumbled, "Hardly. Though history has surprises in store for a lucky few."

"It's just so wondrous to find out that you actually mean something, or your past, where you come from. It makes life somehow feel…special, I guess."

"Surprising effect, isn't it?"

Harper cherished these moments most of all and lounged with his thick hands set behind his head. The squalid, wood paneled room that was his office seemed to grow out of its gloomy and cheaply furnished state, and life itself, which was fashioned for Daryl Harper in much the same manner, held a sort of satisfaction and level of accomplishment that for the first 45 years of his life remained completely absent.

Mrs. Eriksen was grabbing for the ancestral report again, but Harper beat her to it and dropped his thumb on top, keeping her from retrieving the folder.

The middle-aged woman was perplexed at first and stared defiantly at Harper. She got lost in the dark pools of his eyes.

"Your last payment, Mrs. Eriksen," he needled gently.

She immediately retrieved her purse from the dusty floor and plucked several bills from a pearl-beaded wallet. She stared doe eyed at the cunning man, who was as lax and confidant as ever.

He accepted the money with deep satisfaction and almost set to counting it right in front of her in a sort of forgetful greediness.

She watched him ease the money into the top drawer of his desk.

"It's all there," she suggested gently before rocking forward and nabbing the dossier. She clung to it like a delicate artifact, a personal bible of all the promise that a name holds and the way such things are vanquished by the ruinous nature of time.

"I guess our business is through then," he suggested with an air of vexation.

She remained nonetheless, looking like a pathetic and wounded creature in the drained, dusty light of the office. She was a perfectly delicate bird, hollowed out by the years. Her frazzled hair showed strands of gray and though she wore expensive clothes they looked antiquated, funeral-like. And if she had been wearing a bonnet, Harper would've perhaps charged her less.

"Mr. Harper…Daryl," she muttered. The aging biddy lifted her chin a bit, but wouldn't meet his gaze. She turned a few pages in the folder. "You've given me such an amazing gift. I truly appreciate your hard work. You're a…well, a good man. A gentleman. It's a rare thing to find and your interests are so similar to mine, I'd love to take some time to talk about it. This isn't the sort of thing that seems significant to a lot of people, but it is. We both know it, don't we?"

This was the worst part. When the clientele suddenly thought they were Harper's newfound friend, or visa versa. He chalked it up to the personal nature of the business. You dig up the old bones of another's origin and all of a sudden your histories are intertwined. Harper had little understanding and no patience for people. It was easier to deal with the ones that were already gone. And that was the type of racket that would never run itself dry.

She continued to speak. "I'd love to hear about your process and how – "

"I'm busy with the rest of the day, Mrs. Eriksen."

He was tired of putting on airs for this forsaken doll of a woman. He stood swiftly, startling Mrs. Eriksen in her chair, and came around his large desk impatiently.

Sensing his intention, she rose sullenly with the report tucked under her arm. "You're right. I'm sorry. I'm getting carried away."

"Nonsense," he said through clenched teeth.

She turned suddenly and Harper caught a flash of the beauty that had long since betrayed her. "I just never felt…complete, I suppose. Maybe I shouldn't be sharing this with you. But I couldn't make sense of my, well, feeling like I could never settle in. Perhaps its because I was never given a castle." She laughed a sad, pathetic laugh. "I think you've helped me understand."

60

"We all have our rights over the past, Mrs. Eriksen. It's the building blocks of everything—from people, to nature, to society. Those kinds of mysteries are a burden and I hope," he said, reaching out and tugging the corner of the dossier, "that my work's shined some light on whatever doubts, shortcomings, or troubles you've had."

She was now allowing him to usher her towards the exit, though clearly not feeling the need to keep quiet. "I'm not the only one, right?"

"Of course not. A lot of people find this process freeing."

She paused in the open door just as Mr. Harper was trying to ease her out. "Has it ever worked the other way? Has knowing condemned any poor soul?"

"Not so far ma'm. The more we know the better we feel. Genealogy helps us understand our condition. And perhaps you know now why you've felt so cheated in your own."

"Maybe I shouldn't feel that way," she suggested from the hall.

"But I know you do," he said harshly and slammed the door.

It was a relief to be alone and Harper took in the little peace he was afforded. Trudging about the slanted floor, he moved past the string of filing cabinets and snatching Mrs. Eriksen's case file from his desk, tucked it neatly amongst the thousands of others, before jamming the steel drawer shut.

The man staggered back, caught himself on the lip of his desk, and buried his face in his hands. He smelled cigarettes and musk and finally reached out, flipping open his laptop. Harper checked his calendar, reacquainting himself with his next few clients. He scoured the Internet for some insight into the wild and famous pasts that he'd concocted for those appointments. Getting his facts straight, he eased the laptop shut and searched out his cigarettes.

Smoke filled the fusty room, which was already choked with dust, a hint of mildew, and Harper's cologne. He cherished these familiar quarters and looked them up and down pleasantly like he had every day since that bit of good fortune fell into his lap.

Harper's office was a third story cubby set in the heart of the seedy business district. The majority of the renters were loan sharks and all manner of miscreants that used the facilities as sketchy fronts. Daryl Harper fit in well amongst them. It was certainly the perfect environment for D & D Ancestry. The last three years had been prosperous, especially for an unlicensed business owner who never had a proper education.

The memory of where he had come from and where he was now struck Mr. Harper. He smiled savagely and felt the long, jagged scar running along his flabby chin line. He paced for a time, before finally sinking down in his desk chair and rolling towards the window. He smoked and admired the city in its ruin. Rows of stalwart buildings leaned over the avenues like the grubby streets wanted to swallow themselves. At night, the borough was something to behold, lawless and exciting, though it paled in comparison during the day. It almost seemed normal or civilized in the cherry-smoked afternoon. He lost himself to the sounds and smells of the street vendors and the population, the weepy peddlers and the screeching of brakes that rose up before the inevitable smattering of metal.

Mr. Harper lounged like this for the rest of the afternoon, chain smoking and reminiscing on the hardships he once knew.

Completely losing track of time, he was only brought out of his daydream when the thudding knock came at his door – reminding him of the work at hand.

He stubbed out his cigarette and flicking it from the window, set with long stride across the office. Sidling up to the door, he threw back the lock and poked his head out into the dreary hallway.

"Mr. Hastings, yeah?"

The squeamish runt looked about, startled. "This is D & D Ancestry, correct?"

"Sure is," Harper said invitingly and opened up for the man.

62

He didn't enter right away, but commenced to scan the dingy suite. "Cause there's no signs outside or even on the door."

He clapped the man's scrawny shoulder. "Well we're big on privacy. Some are concerned with keeping the history of family matters to themselves. Celebrities and the like."

"Really?" Mr. Hastings muttered in awe, allowing himself to be ushered into the office.

"Of course," Harper claimed haphazardly. "Now why don't we begin?" Then he shut the door and the whole charade started again.

The day wound itself out dully, forcing Mr. Harper to put on quite the front. He always got sleepy late in the afternoon as the stories and peoples' naivety wore themselves out. Some were more gullible than others and Harper had to measure each job carefully to ensure that no man or woman left with even the slightest doubt. Some were prone to fame, some to more humbled histories, and Harper had gotten quite good at reading his clientele, knowing what they were after and what would satisfy their unsuspecting curiosities. Callow and wide-eyed and miserable people filed in and out and he gave them exactly what they needed: a grander sense of being. They wanted to feel important, higher born, bigger than whatever was possible here and now. They longed for fantasy, for a life they could claim some kinship to in order to overcome the malaise and finite prospects of ordinary existence.

Mr. Harper was only too glad to finish the last appointment for the day and when the proprietor finally found himself alone, he set to his favorite chore, which was counting the money.

Slipping off his shoes and unbuttoning his shirt, Harper fell into a kind of stupor as he smoked and tallied everything up. After a while, he broke his concentration and dug an apple from his desk. Slicing away slivers with the nifty switchblade he kept tucked in his pocket; he slowly rounded out the day.

Dusk arrived in a bevvy of copper hues, giving a stale and depleted look to the neighborhood and Mr. Harper's dwelling. He listened to the building settle in the dry heat and watched the sunset from his window before packing up for the evening.

There was little on his mind, drained as he was from the hours of humoring countless lost and desperate people.

Just as Harper was setting his desk in order, he was struck by the sneaking suspicion that someone was outside his office. Peering up, he caught a shadow darkening the threshold and he preternaturally sensed the presence in the hall. There was a knock and Harper sat there silently, hoping that the lifelessness of the place would ward them off. But when the second knock came ever more demanding, Harper tucked the money away and standing at his desk, hollered, "We only see people by appointment. And we're closed for the day."

The doorknob wiggled, alarming Harper, who didn't have the slightest clue why anyone would be that demanding or impetuous concerning the genealogy trade.

"Mr. Harper, I'd like to speak to you."

The man sounded neither menacing nor rushed, but Harper felt the pangs of uncertainty nonetheless. "Call my secretary in the morning and make an appointment."

"You don't have a secretary, Mr. Harper. Now would you please make this easy on the both of us and open the door."

The proprietor remained apprehensive. He thought a moment, rapping his fingers over the desk in succession. Rising, he kicked his chair back and moseyed up to the door.

"What's your business here?" he hollered through the crack.

"Nothing out of the ordinary. Just checking in."

This struck Harper as even more suspicious and he felt for the switchblade as he asked, "For who?"

"The leasing company that owns the building."

64

"I been paying on time."

"It's nothing like that. We're just doin' annual check ups, makin' sure the places are kept properly."

Against his better judgment, Harper unlocked the door and edged it open just enough to get a look at the stranger.

He was a jackal of a man, sharp eyed and baleful. Despite appearing prim in his expensive suit, Harper knew a muscleman when he saw one. Those big, scarred hands the youth kept folded before him were telling enough.

"Today's no good," Harper spat, but it was too late to swing the door shut. The stranger's boot was neatly tucked in its path.

"Just a word," he said through cracked teeth. He leaned forward and cocked one eye to the side, leering in like a wolf hungry for prey.

Without an option, Harper scooted back quickly and let the door fall open of its own accord.

"Well then," the stranger grumbled as he sashayed in.

Harper watched him carefully, not making any bold moves, yet keeping his hand wrapped tight around the blade in his pocket.

The young, sturdy man thumbed his nose and said, "I should be honest. I might've overstated my purpose here."

Putting a safe distance between himself and the gutsy stranger, Harper asked, "Then who sent you?"

The man paced the floor, giving a satisfied nod as he observed the dull space. "I'm here on behalf of some business associates. It's come to our attention that you've been running this company for several years now, and quite successfully at that."

"Why's that anybody else's business?" The men were squaring up, trying to gauge the other's intention.

The stranger kicked past the shabby rug, fiddling about the countertop and amongst the row of filing cabinets. "We just figured its important to extend our well wishes to successful people and offer any services they might need in the future."

65

"What do I look like to you?"

"Please, Mr. Harper. Everyone's happy you finally found your niche after struggling for so many years in the neighborhood. Our demands aren't unreasonable. We have too much respect for a man who's built himself up."

With a huff, Harper swung to one side of the room and leaned against the windowsill. "Hellof'a shakedown."

"We just feel its right to share such good fortune."

Harper frowned, trying to prepare himself for anything. "I think you got this all wrong."

"Let's not pretend. This is quite the regular little racket you got going for yourself."

Harper drew forward, heatedly. "I don't take kindly to threats."

"This isn't a threat, Mr. Harper. So you can let go of that knife in your pocket and relax. I'm here to make this easy."

"Yeah, and how much is that gonna cost me?"

"Nothing exorbitant," he claimed with a peevish glance.

Growing tetchy, Harper eyed the street outside and muttered, "Well I'll tell you now, I'm not sure there's much to be made shaking down a businessman like myself."

The man gave a frightening laugh that sounded like rusty nails shaken in a tin can. "A businessman? I'll give you this, you do have quite the sense of humor."

There was nothing Harper hated more than getting treated like a chump. Myriad thoughts welled in his mind, each growing bloodier by the second. He ambled his way over to the desk and began to fret over the knickknacks there.

Reading his obstinacy, the stranger started in again. "This is an opportunity for you. It will ensure that you can continue to operate without any unforeseen issues."

"Like what?"

"Plenty can befall a man, his place of business. We watch out for you. Make sure that none of this meets some unforeseen misfortune. The same services are provided for you, of course."

"You ever been cut on?"

"Excuse me?"

"Ever been cornered? Ya' ever been forced to grow fierce and lash out?"

"Are we talking figuratively here?" he said, trying to maintain his strained humor.

Harper shot him a dangerous look, then plucked the switchblade from his pocket and set it down roughly on the desk. He took pleasure in the fact that it brought a small rise out of the man. "I've known people to grow vicious in those straits," Harper assured him.

The man sized Harper up thoughtfully, before turning his attention to the office. "So what is it exactly that you do here? I hope it's a bit more exciting than it seems."

Harper stood his ground.

Surprisingly, the man turned his back on Harper and began to peruse his files. "Is it the fraud that's exhilarating? I mean it must take some effort to come up with all these lies you sell to people."

"I let them believe what they want."

"But they are forged." He plucked a few files loose and began scanning their pages. "I mean it's all a bit of tall tales, a mock up, fraud."

Harper crossed his arms and turned, hiding his look of frustration in the shadows. "I report on what I can about peoples lineage. Sometimes you've got to put a spin on reality."

"How thrilling. And let's say the police were let in on your little con."

Harper grimaced, trying to keep his cool. Already, beads of sweat were showing on his forehead and his hands were growing clammy. "I'm as legitimate as any of the other companies."

The stranger's curt laugh interrupted Harper again. "C'mon, let's have the truth. You're no more than a thug in a ripped off suit."

67

"You sure got a lot to say," Harper mouthed and suddenly leapt into action. Retrieving his switchblade, he snapped the knife open, swinging wildly toward his assailant, who was already two steps ahead of him. The stranger kicked out Harper's foot and tucked the barrel of a berretta under his chin.

They shared a perilous glance as Harper held the knife out at his side.

"Don't be a fool," the stranger began. "The intention isn't to hurt you. And I don't think either of us wants to shed blood today."

Harper glowered with a fierce animalism. His thoughts were all frayed and his senses askew. He just felt the blood rushing hot through his veins and a pervading lust for violence.

"Easy now," the stranger suggested with a nod. He teased Harper's chin with the muzzle.

Harper slowly set the knife on the edge of his desk. "What now?"

The man backed away, looking less grave, though he kept the gun trained on Harper. "Do what's best and keep right on working how you have."

Harper just glared and nodded.

The stranger backed up through the ever-darkening room and finally hid the handgun away. "See, we can all be reasonable."

"If you say so," Harper griped.

The young man nodded, taking in his surroundings one last time. He looked even more dangerous as the last light of day drained from the office. "The first payment is due in a week. Just think of us as partners." Then with a swift turn, he headed toward the exit.

Struggling to reclaim his nerve, Harper croaked, "You never said who you work for."

The man paused in the lightless doorway. He looked over his shoulder with a hint of pleasure, muttering, "No...I didn't," before disappearing with weighty tread down the hall.

Harper stood stark still in the office, trying to take it all in. At the same time he was listening to ensure the stranger's footsteps were drifting away. He felt frayed and cowardly and most of all frustrated over his own inaction. Then again, he didn't have any other option. Even if he had flayed the kid, who's to say a nastier brute wouldn't come and take his place.

Exacerbated, the lowly proprietor nabbed his switchblade from the desk and hurried towards the door, where he threw both deadbolts, though he still felt eerily vulnerable.

Floundering through the room, Harper turned on the desk lamp and sank down in his chair, worn out from another long day in a life where no one is spared – past, present, or future

.

***

© 2017 Ehren Baker

Burning Snow

by Morgan Boyd

I was pissing away the last of my cash on shots
and beers in South Madison at The Moccasin when a
fat man with a cracked red face and long gray hair sat
next to me. Removing his coat, he revealed a faded
tie-dyed Grateful Dead T-shirt. After laughing at a
Geico commercial on the TV behind the bar, he
ordered a shot and a beer.

"Name's Mark," he said.

"Max," I replied.

I'd been in The Berkshires just long enough to slip
on the ice and bust my ass. At first, I enjoyed the
snow. Big fluffy flakes swirling through the air like the
Christmas holiday's of my youth, but after a few
freezing days, my winter wonderland transformed into
a vast expanse of cruddy gray post-apocalyptic tundra.

"Funny thing 'bout a bar," Mark said. "Two
strangers sittin' next to each other's buddies after a
beer."

Mark bantered on about this and that, and I threw
in the obligatory head nod or 'uh-huh' without paying
much attention to the conversation. When my beer
bottomed out, I reached for my coat.

"Lookin' for a job?" Mark asked. "Shovelin' snow.
Could use the help. Ain't runway modelin'. Pays the
minimum under the table."

Mark picked me up at my motel room the next day,
and we drove to a large house with a long snow
covered driveway near the college. He let me out the
truck, and said he'd be back in an hour. I shoveled and
salted the drive like a bland dinner until a 4x4 with a
loud muffler and a snowplow attached to the front
stopped across the street. Two heavyset men in
parkas and Boston Red Sox caps climbed from the
cab.

"You with Mark?" The driver asked.

"We ain't dating," I said.

"This guy being funny?" The passenger asked.

"Wish you'd showed up earlier," I said motioning to the plow attached to the front of their truck. "Could have saved me some serious work."

They lit cigarettes, and talked amongst themselves before returning to their vehicle. The 4x4 rumbled into the front yard, and plowed a heap of snow onto the driveway. The big guys in the truck flipped me off, and flung snow and ice at me with the truck's back tires before driving away.

Another car stopped before the driveway as I started in on the fresh mess. A tall slender young woman with long black hair, radiant blue eyes, and pale white skin exited a gold Saturn.

"What happened?" She asked.

"Couple guys got hungry, made a doughnut in the yard."

"Name's Renee."

"Max."

She went inside the house, and returned with a snow shovel. I said it wasn't necessary, but she insisted. I certainly didn't mind the view or the attention.

"Parents' place?" I asked.

"Renting a room. Student at South Madison State." Mark honked from the street.

"Why's she helpin'?" He asked.

"Wanted to."

"Why aint you done yet?"

"Couple guys with a plow took it upon themselves to return the snow I'd shoveled to its original resting place."

"Dammit," Mark said. "Hop in."

"Want to grab coffee sometime?" Renee asked when I waved bye.

"Very much so," I said.

"Saturday at the Appalachian Grind," she said. "10:00AM."

"See you there," I said, and climbed into the cab, trying to suppress a smile.

72

"The Brown Brothers," Mark said at the Moccasin. "Also own a snow removal business. Miserable little shits. Mike Brown Sr.'s their dad, richest son-of-a-bitch in South Madison. Owns the Mountainside Bar and Grill up in Lewisburg."

"How's the steak?" I asked.

"You aint heard of the Mountainside Bar and Grill? Afterhours parties in the basement, naked women, cocaine, orgies, bondage that sort of thing."

"And they're muscling you out of the snow?" I asked.

"Tryin' to," Mark said with a shrug, revealing a handgun tucked under his shirt. "Mike Jr.'s the fatter of the two brothers, but Toby's also a lardass. You should see their dad. Fattest fuck there ever was."

He went on and on about what creeps the Brown's were, but I didn't care. The situation was some ticky-tacky Mickey Mouse bullshit that smacked of preteens fighting for the right to trim Ms. O'Malley's bush for a quarter. I went along with what Mark was saying without paying much attention, and didn't say no when he offered to buy the next round.

The next morning somebody knocked on my motel room door. I yelled that I didn't need room service, but the banging continued, so I stumbled out of bed.

"Hurry up Max," Mark said. "Snow ain't shovelin' itself. We got work to do."

I dragged myself into the bathroom, and splashed water on my face. In the cab, Mark handed me a box of doughnuts and a lukewarm coffee.

"This the job?" I asked in front of an aging apartment complex.

"Grabbin' Jolly," Mark said and honked.

A little guy with long greasy brown hair and a tangled beard limped to the truck. I slid over, noticing his swollen nose and blackened eyes.

"Jolly meet Max," Mark said.

We said hello, and drove into Madison. South Madison was a bedraggled string of closed factories and low income housing, but Madison was an upscale example of what the founding fathers had in mind.

Pristine three-story brick mansions lined both sides of the street.

Mark left us at the worksite with shovels and salt. Jolly didn't say much, and I was okay with that, but I was curious about his stupid name, and his recently punched face.

We shoveled our butts off until Mark returned with McDonald's for lunch, and drove away again. I lit a smoke, and Jolly bummed one.

"What happened to your face?" I asked, deciding I didn't care about the origin of his name.

"Shoveling ain't all rainbows and unicorns," he said.

"Should I start worrying about the abominable snowman?" I asked.

"Just the Brown Brothers."

"Ran into them yesterday," I said. "Rich brats trying to edge Mark out the snow game. Their daddy owns a bar up the mountain."

"Bad shit goes down at the Mountainside," Jolly said. "Couple of college girls ended up missing there last year. Let me get another cigarette?"

"Want my wallet too?" I asked, opening my pack.

"Brown boys are rumored to have ties," Jolly said, lighting the smoke. "What'd you say you used to do?"

"I didn't."

I told Jolly I was a carpenter, flipping houses in Utah, but the work dried up after the crash. None of it was true.

I expected The Brown Brothers to show up and protest our shoveling, but they never did. Neither did our employer. Jolly called Mark's cellphone, but he didn't answer. After waiting in the cold for an hour, we walked toward South Madison. Traversing brown slush on the side of the road, Jolly stuck out his thumb at the passing cars until somebody stopped. The truck was equipped with a gun rack, and the driver wore a camouflage ball cap.

"Thanks for the ride, Howard," Jolly said. "Mark's M.I.A."

"I was drinkin' with him at the Moccasin," Howard said. "Brown Brothers showed. Mark bought 'em

74

drinks, and they poured 'em on his head, dragged him outside, and pistol-whipped him with his own gun. Broke his arm too."

"Why didn't you do something?" Jolly asked.

"You know how it is," Howard said.

After the *Dunkin' Donuts* drive thru, Howard dropped me off at my motel. I was tired and sore, so I ate an egg and steak bagel, and drifted off to sleep, watching Sports Center.

I dreamt Gunnar was driving through a snowstorm in the Las Vegas desert. I sat in the passenger seat, pleading for my life. He pulled over in the middle of nowhere, dragged me from the car, and made me dig my own grave in the snow. When I finished the hole, Gunnar shot me in the gut, and I fell backwards into my last resting place. The falling snowflakes turned to cinders as Gunnar shoveled burning snow into the pit.

I woke in a cold sweat, kicking off the blanket. A morning show was on the TV, so I turned it off. I jumped out of bed because I was late for coffee with Renee. I splashed water on my face, and combed my hair. Fragments of the nightmare lingered in my mind when I arrived at the *Appalachian Grind*.

"Thought you stood me up," Renee said, wearing a low cut blouse and tight pants.

"You want a croissant or something?" I asked.

"Double Americano with room," she said.

Over steaming drinks, she told me she was from upstate New York, and a junior in the accounting program at the college. I gave her the standard flipping houses in Utah routine when it came time for me to share.

We smoked along Main Street. Churches and real estate offices peppered the strip. Other flavors included a cinema, a playhouse and a bookshop. We stopped at the war memorial, and Renee kissed me. Back at my motel room, we ordered a pizza after sex, and stretched out in bed, naked, smoking and watching shitty television. Some Bogart films were playing at the local cinema, so we dressed, and saw a double feature, but didn't catch much of either film. In

75

the evening, she had to study for an exam, and kissed me goodbye.

I woke early the next day, feeling rested, and ready to shovel the shit out of some snow. Mark never arrived, so I walked to the Moccasin, hoping to find him on a barstool.

"Seen Mark?" I asked Howard.

"Imagine he's laid up, high as pitch pine" Howard said. "Poor bastard needs to tough it out though, and shovel some drives before the melt."

"I'll do it for him," I said.

"Good man," Howard said, and bought me a shot and a beer.

We stopped at Jolly's after drinks, and Howard honked.

Jolly climbed in the truck, and lit a crack pipe. Howard took a hit. They offered me the glass, but I declined. A snow covered swing set and various large children's toys sat abandoned in Mark's front yard. A woman with a child on her hip and another hanging from her dress answered the door.

"Afternoon Diane," Howard said. "Came to check on Mark."

"He's asleep," she said.

"Got a couple boys want to shovel for him while he's on the mend."

"Come on in."

The living room was beat to shit, covered in stains and crayon. Mark lumbered into the room with a bandaged forehead, and an arm sling.

"Mornin'," he said, glassy-eyed.

"These boys want to work," Howard said.

"Job at Anderson's cabin," Mark slurred.

"Lewisburg. I know it," Howard said. "Grab your shovels. Let's get movin'."

The road was steep. I thought we'd spin out on the incline, but the snow tires gripped like Velcro. At the Anderson's cabin, Howard left us with the shovels and salt. Amazing how drudgery seems like leisure when you've got a woman on your mind. Work clipped along. Jolly hit the pipe every twenty minutes.

76

Anderson's neighbor complimented us, and asked if we'd shovel his driveway too. Jolly wanted to go home, but I said yes.

About halfway through the second job, a familiar 4x4 pulled into the driveway. The Brown Brothers exited the truck with baseball bats. Jolly fled behind the Anderson's neighbor's cabin. Can't say I blamed him. He was pretty frail.

"Thought we made it clear, we don't want you shoveling 'round here," Mike Jr. said.

"Plenty snow to go around," I said.

"Let's see if you're still a funny guy after batting practice," Toby said.

Mike Jr. swung his bat. I dodged the blow, and jabbed him in the throat with the shovel blade. Mike Jr. doubled over, wheezing and gurgling. I parried Toby's swing, throwing him off balance. He slipped and fell on his ass. I clocked him hard in the face with the spade. Mike Jr. and Toby slowly got to their feet, and limped to the 4x4.

"You're fucking dead," Toby said.

I lit a cigarette, and waved bye.

"Thought your ass was beat for sure," Jolly said, returning to the front yard. "You whoop 'em?"

"Yep," I said, and took a drag.

"Better watch out," Jolly said. "They're connected."

I was walking to the Appalachian Grind to meet Renee Saturday morning when I saw him coming out of a bank on Main Street. It couldn't be, but it was. I'd recognize that son-of-a-bitch anywhere. How the hell did Gunnar know I was alive—let alone halfway across the country in Podunk South Madison?

I returned to my motel room, and packed my clothes and .45. I could borrow Mark's truck, and be out of town in under an hour. Somebody knocked. I held my gun at the hip, peeking out the window.

"What the fuck Max," Renee said. "You never showed. Now I find you here with your thumb up your ass."

"Thanks for the fun Renee, but I'm the fuck 'em and chuck 'em type," I said.

77

She slapped my face, and slammed the door.

I felt bad, but it was for the best. I lit a smoke, and started for Mark's house through slushy brown streets. A truck flashed its lights. I reached for my gun.

"Where you been Max?" Howard said. "Got bad news. Jolly's mom found him dead, drug overdose."

"Damn," I said.

"Heading to Mark's? Hop in."

Thick black smoke filled the sky.

Mark, Diane and their kids stood in the front yard watching their house burn. Mark's truck was engulfed in flames too. Howard hopped out, leaving the keys in the ignition, so I slid into the driver's seat. I felt bad for Mark and Jolly like maybe I was partially to blame for this mess, but not bad enough to stick around.

"Step outside," Gunnar said through the window, holding a pistol level with my face.

Gunnar disarmed me, and we climbed into the Brown Brother's 4x4. At The Mountainside Bar And Grill, they escorted me through a back door, down a set of stairs, and into a small damp room. Gunnar cracked me on the head with the butt of his gun, and I went limp.

I came to, strapped to a wooden chair, my head throbbing. The basement walls vibrated with techno music.

"Johnny Hall," Gunnar said. "What the hell you doing in shithole town U.S.A.?"

"I grew up in this shithole town," Toby said.

"No offense," Gunnar said, sticking a knife blade up my nose. "But this ain't exactly Vegas. You pissing off the wrong people again Johnny. Only you could rise from the grave, and botch a second chance."

A door opened, revealing a blinding light.

"This ain't the bathroom," Toby yelled at somebody, and the door shut.

The blade sliced through my nostril. Blood spurted in time with the pain.

The basement walls melted into my darkened Nevada desert grave. I loosened an arm from under the sand enough to dig out my other arm, and then my face. Stars twinkled overhead as I freed myself. The gunshot wound in my gut leaked, but nothing vital seemed damaged. I walked in moonlight until I saw the neon glow of Las Vegas in the distance.

"Who the hell is it?" Stacey asked from within when I reached her apartment, and knocked on the door. "Johnny, oh my god. Come in. You look like dog shit on fire. What happened?"

Stacey was a stripper I sometimes crashed with. I'd helped her out of enough pickles, and given her enough money when she was in need to know I could trust her. She took me in, cleaned me up, and dressed my wound.

"You better dip Johnny," Stacey said after I told her Gunnar had buried me alive for ripping him off. "He'll never stop trying to kill you if he finds out you're still alive."

Stacy gave me a ride to the depot, and I boarded the first leviathan out of town. The basement walls, the techno music and the horrible pain in my nose reanimated. I sat alone in the darkness. Through a purple gloom, a door opened. The silhouette of a woman twinkled with a thousand tiny constellations.

"Max?" A celestial voice whispered, untying my wrists and legs. "Let's get you out of here."

"Stacy?" I asked as she led me up the stairs, and out the back door.

"Who's Stacy? I have to get back before they notice," Renee said, her body shimmering with glitter in the moonlight as she descended the stairs.

I staggered toward the tree line at the edge of the parking lot. Angry voices emanated behind me, followed by gunshots. I disappeared into the forest, and stopped to catch my breath. My side burned, and blood smeared my hand when I touched my waist.

"Come back Johnny," Gunnar said from the parking lot. "Got your lady friend. Come back or we'll feed her to Mike Sr."

The snow was deep. The cold brought back my senses. I stayed out of sight in the trees, trying not to think about my wounds, or what Gunnar meant by feeding Renee to the Brown boy's dad. Hypothermia was setting in as I reached the Moccasin. My mutilated face was blue and my teeth rattled like a trestle. Howard and Mark sat at the end of the bar. Mark's head lay on the counter, surrounded by a traffic jam of empty shot glasses.

"What the hell happened?" Howard asked.

"He can't be in here looking like that," the bartender said.

Howard threw cash on the bar, and dragged Mark from the tavern to his truck. I cranked on the heater.

"Brown Brothers give you that nose job?" Howard asked.

"What do you know about Mike Sr.?"

"Has a penchant for the college girls. Rumored to be into some kinky shit. He was a suspect when those two women went missing. Never found 'em either. You want a ride to the hospital?"

"A woman I know is in trouble," I said. "I need a gun."

Howard nodded, and drove us to his house. Animal busts hung on the walls. Mark snored on the couch. Howard gave me a roll of gauze.

"You kill these animals?" I asked.

"Most of 'em," he said. "Pops got a few."

"Live alone?" I asked.

"Wife left about a year ago. It was drinking or her. Easy choice. Get that tape on your nose. Tired of looking at your busted face."

Howard led me into a backroom.

"This here's a .30-06 Springfield," he said. "I can wipe a buck's ass from a thousand yards with this bad boy. Take this Russian AEK-971 assault rifle, and this M9 Beretta. Put this .38 in your boot."

"Why you doing this for me?" I asked.

"Jolly didn't die from an overdoes, and Mark's place didn't burn down by accident. Brown's been terrorizing South Madison for far too long. We've needed a crazy son-of-a-bitch like you to come along, and clean house for some time."

"Got any gas?" I asked.

80

On the drive, we didn't talk. My mind wandered to pancakes and coffee at an all night dinner on the Vegas strip.

"Pass the syrup," Fred said. "You're paler than a ghost. First kill is always the hardest. It gets easier from here on out. Second nature."

"You don't think any less of me 'cause I puked?" I asked.

"Hell no," he laughed. "If memory serves, I chunked my first time too. The thing you need to understand now is that by killing that man you've signed your own death certificate."

"What?"

"There's now a bullet with your name on it. Natural progression of the trade," Fred said. "I got one with my name on it too."

A few months later, Fred's prophecy came true, and his bullet found its way through his temple, during a botched bank robbery.

A truck idled in the middle of the road after the turnoff to the Mountainside Bar and Grill. Two men leaned against the hood. I hid in the back of the cab.

"Evening boys," Howard said, rolling down the window. "Why you in the middle of the road?"

"None of your goddamn business," one of the men said, shining a flashlight at Howard's face. "What you doing here?"

"Hoping to grab a burger, and a side of pussy," Howard said.

"Restaurant's closed," the man said. "Step out the truck."

"Why?" Howard asked.

"Just step the fuck out," the man said pointing a gun at Howard.

I sat up, and fired four shots through the window. Both men dropped to the ground, each with two bullet holes in the forehead.

"Jesus Christ," Howard said.

"Where?" I asked.

We drove around the dead men and their truck. In the restaurant's parking lot somebody opened fire. I ducked out of the cab with the guns and gas can. A hail of gunfire blasted through the restaurant's front window. A bullet struck my shoulder. I opened fire with the assault rifle, and made my way through the front door.

The bar was empty, so I poured gasoline over the counter, and lit a match. A bullet nicked my ear. I walked into the kitchen. Mike Jr. fumbled with a jammed pistol. I raised the M9 to his head, and heat ripped through my lower back, followed by a deafening crack, lightening before thunder. I dropped to my knees.

"I'll kill you a thousand times if I have to," Gunnar said, putting a gun to my head.

"Stop burring me alive, and you won't have to," I said as the flames ate away at the ceiling.

"See you in hell Johnny," Gunnar said as the flames found the gas line, and an exploding fireball knocked us off our feet.

The roof collapsed, and burning debris crashed down around me. I sat up, looking for Gunnar as snowflakes fell through the hole in the roof, mingling with the flames. Through the smoke, I saw Gunnar's body lying on the floor. His head crushed under a blazing wooden beam.

Crawling beneath thick black smoke, I made my way down the stairs into the basement, passing several tables and a stripper pole. I found Renee tied to a board, and covered in lacerations. A massive naked fat man with clothespins clipped to his nipples and genitals held a knife to Renee's throat. He was a spitting image of his boys only older, and fatter—much fatter. The fire ate away at the walls.

"Drop the knife asshole," I said, pointing the M9 at Mike Sr.

He stabbed Renee in the gut as I unloaded my weapon.

Mike Sr. collapsed in a fat heap of bullet holes on the floor. Renee screamed in agony as I untied her. Smoke and flames filled the room. We stumbled up the backstairs into the snow.

My breathing grew shallow. The restaurant was completely engulfed in flames. Several sharp pains ripped through my chest. I went down on my knees as I saw the Brown Brothers approaching with rifles.

More gunshots sounded, and I realized there was crossfire. Toby went down, and Mike Jr. dragged him behind a car. The barrel of a .30-06 peeked from the window of Howard's truck across the parking lot. Mike Jr. returned fire, and Howard slumped over the steering wheel onto the horn.

Renee helped me to my feet, and we stumbled into the tree line. Blood stained the snow behind us as we staggered through the drift. At a small clearing, we rested on a fallen log.

I sank into Renee's arms.

"I strip to help pay for college," Renee said.

"I knew there was something I liked about you," I said, and a gunshot knocked her off the log.

"Toby's dead," Mike Jr. said, covered in blood, and holding a pistol.

"So is your pervert dad."

He raised his gun as I pulled the .38 from my boot, and sent Mike Jr. across the river Styx to join his family as a bullet from his gun named Johnny Hall tore through my chest.

Moonlight illuminated Renee's body. The glitter on her breasts twinkled through the blood like a thousand tiny stars across a red sky. I crawled through the snow, and kissed her blue lips as though she would wake, and we'd live happily ever after, but this ain't no fairytale.

***

The Lioness Must Hunt

by Calvin Demmer

Bella Rossi ripped the tape off Officer Dave Reed's mouth. He winced in pain and called her a "bitch." She waved him off, inhaling the stench of sweat that hung in the motel room as the morning light pierced through gaps in the turquoise blinds. Bella buttoned up her white shirt, choosing to forego putting on her bra, which she placed in her black handbag. Stalking back to the bed, she glanced at Officer Reed's naked body, before focusing on the handcuffs that kept him bound to the headboard.

"Un-cuff me," Officer Reed demanded. "I've got to get ready for work."

"Work?" Bella chuckled. "I'm so fortunate to have a wealthy husband.

"That's great for you. I, on the other hand, have to get going."

Bella picked up the leather whip on the bed next to Officer Reed. "First, let's have a little lesson before I go."

"Huh?"

She cracked the whip, hitting the pillow to the left of his face. "You want a lesson?"

"Ah, I guess. One little lesson can't be bad. I've been a bad boy, after all."

"Is that so?" Bella rested her left knee on the mattress.

"I've been very, very bad."

Bella's eyes hardened. "The male lion with his large, proud mane is known as the 'King of the Jungle,' and is classified as an apex predator. However, it's not the male lion you should fear when lost in the wild, for there is another, quicker, deadlier, and more cerebral killer that roams the land. Do you know which animal it is?"

"Ah, fuck, a bear?"

85

"Wrong." Bella brought the whip down across the man's chest. The slash sound heightened her senses. Looking down, she saw she'd drawn blood.

"Goddamn, you're crazy bitch. What the fuck was that for?"

"The correct answer is *the lioness.* Not only does she care for the young, but along with other lionesses, she stalks the lands, hidden in her surroundings until she's ready to strike. As she and her pride of lionesses encircle you, you realize there is no escape. The alpha female has you. You feel her claws rip through your skin, and her teeth pry down on limbs no longer yours."

"You fucking cut me. I'm bleeding."

"It's at this point you would wish you'd have rather run into the male lion. He's slower and prefers spending his days sleeping in the shade. Sound familiar?"

"Fuck you." Officer Reed pulled on the handcuffs. "Let me go now, or I'll arrest you. If I'd known you were some psycho, I wouldn't have banged your brains out last night."

"Hardly." Bella chuckled.

She held the whip as if she was going to strike again. Officer Reed grimaced and turned his head. No blow came. Instead, Bella placed the whip in her handbag, picked it up, and made her way towards the bathroom. She snorted a line of the cocaine on the cream-colored counter and returned to the room. "Bye," she said, waving to Officer Reed. "Enjoy you work."

Bella exited the motel room, ignoring his swearing and antics on the bed.

She had better places to be.

*

Bella sat with two of her friends, Kristy and Sienna, at their favorite table at the country club. In front of her stood a cocktail with an extra dash of vodka. She glanced up at the two middle-aged men playing tennis on the court. The three of them often mocked and laughed at the club's male members when they played tennis. They never made a move on any of the attractive men, as they'd agreed on a rule to never hunt too close to home.

"So," Sienna said, running her hand through her glimmering red hair, "I have something to show you two."

"Go on, then," Bella said.

Sienna lifted her white top, revealing a small tattoo just below one of her breasts of a snake curling around an apple. "Isn't it beautiful?"

"Looks amazing," Kristy said.

Bella, noticing Sienna wasn't wearing a bra, glanced to her left and caught the barman transfixed on her friend. She turned back to Sienna. "Two hundred dollars says you won't lift your top any farther."

"How much farther?"

"I think you know."

"Three hundred."

"Deal."

Sienna pulled her top up, two perky pale breasts with large pink nipples popped out. Bella turned to the bartender, who was blushing. He turned away, focusing on wiping the bar down with his white cloth. "Now," Sienna said, pulling her top back up. "Can we get on to business?'

Kristy twirled ends of her ash brown hair. She downed her shot of tequila; her light shade of purple lipstick left a mark on the rim of the glass. "I'm on seven."

"Nine," Sienna said.

Bella grinned. "Try twenty-six."

"Twenty-six?" Kristy turned the empty shot glass over. "But that would mean you did three already this week?"

"That's right, I left one this morning, handcuffed in some dodgy motel room."

"I don't know how you do it. I'm so scared my husband will find out. He's been coming home earlier as of late, giving me so little opportunity."

"That sucks." Bella indicated to one of the servers they were ready to order. "Charles leaves at six in the morning and is only back at seven at night. Mama has lots of time to play. It looks like I have this competition in the bag."

"First to thirty it was," Sienna said. "You might have it in the bag by next week. Nice pocket of cash to win. Fifty-grand could buy some wonderful clothes."

"Oh, but that means our game will be over," Kristy said. "What then?"

"Do you have any ideas, Bella?" Sienna asked. "I'm thinking of something. The guys are getting a bit stale. But rest assured ladies, there is always something worth hunting. Who knows? Maybe we'll do women next."

Sienna tapped her arm. "That does sound enticing. We definitely will need something more hardcore, though, to keep me excited."

Kristy said, "More hardcore than cheating on our—" she paused as a server brought their menus.

Bella smiled.

*

Friday night Bella's husband left for a work function. She'd faked a stomach bug, while assuring him she'd be fine and that it would be poor form of him not to show up. Once he was gone, she put on a figure hugging red dress, a pair of black heels, and did her makeup to perfection.

She drove to a cocktail bar on the other side of town that she'd heard of. Seated at the main bar, it didn't take long for her to attract the opposite sex's attention. A middle-aged man with a patchy brown beard, wearing a black bomber jacket and faded jeans, made his way to her.

"Hi, I'm Marty." He reached out for her hand.

"Lily." Bella shook the man's hand, noticing it was rough and dry.

"Can I get you a drink?"

"Sure, that would be great."

Marty wasn't the most attractive man in the bar, especially with the harsh white light shining down over

88

the bar, illuminating his wrinkled face and thinning brown hair, but he had some confidence. Whenever they fell into conversations where he had above average knowledge, his demeanor perked up even more. His old school, rustic charm also had a certain pure swagger absent in the young men Bella had been with. It even reminded her a bit of her husband before he'd gone all corporate and became more obsessed with chasing the green rather than her.

Like throwing a brick through a window, a few drinks shattered any nervous energy, and soon the sexual innuendos flowed. When Bella had her third glass of wine, it was time to get the action started.

"Where are you staying?" she asked.

"Oh, I'm renting an apartment a few miles from here. I'm still looking around for something more permanent."

"Sounds perfect. I'll follow you in my car."

*

Bella handcuffed Marty to the bed. After gagging him and removing his shirt, she reached for the one of the scented candles. The wax sizzled as it dropped onto his bare chest.

Marty moaned.

"After a bit of pain, there shall be great reward." Bella put the candle down and unzipped her dress. It fell to the ground, revealing her tanned, toned body.

"Wow," Marty said.

Once completely naked, Bella sat on the bed alongside Marty, unbuckling his belt. Victory would be hers. Kristy and Sienna had no chance. After Marty, she only needed three more. It would be easy. By this time next week, she would be pocketing the fifty-thousand dollar prize.

But it wasn't just about the money.

She felt alive, really alive.

It was all about the hunt, a necessity she'd deprived herself of for too long.

She kissed Marty's neck and climbed onto him.

A *crash* emanated from behind her.

Turning around, she saw a figure dressed in black from head to toe. This included a black mask that only had two eye holes. A large blade shimmered under the warm yellow light of the room. The intruder came straight for the two of them.

Bella moved just time in time to avoid the blade, which slashed Marty's neck, sending crimson blooding spurting into the air. Warm drops landed on the side of her body. The intruder then stabbed him in the chest. Bella dived onto the floor next to bed, seeking safety. She crawled toward to the bathroom, but found the person in black had rounded the bed.

"Please, don't!" Bella cried.

The intruder pointed the knife at her.

"Please, I'm begging you. I will give you money. I will give you anything you want."

The intruder removed the mask.

"Sienna?"

"That's right." Sienna smiled. "Kristy and I made a new game after you left the club the other day. The one who stops you gets a hundred thousand. I wanted to win to win that last game so badly. Sure, it was fun. But I didn't have sex with those men for nothing. I've never won at anything. I need this."

"Please, Sienna. This isn't the way—"

The left side of Sienna's face exploded, sending flesh and other matter onto the white wall to Bella's right. Sienna crumpled like a newspaper being crunched into a ball. She landed hard on the floor with a thud.

"She's been following you all day," someone said. Bella knew the voice before she'd even turned or gotten to her feet.

"Kristy?"

"I knew she'd make her move tonight to stop you. I couldn't let her win."

"I understand." Bella stood and held her hands up, hoping to calm Kristy. "What do you say we get out of here and go for some drinks?"

"I can't do that." Kristy aimed the gun at her. "I can't let you win the first game, either."

"For fuck's sake, just listen to me." Bella took a step back. "Please, Kristy, I beg you. I'll give you anything you want."

"That's not how it works."

Kristy pulled the trigger twice. With the silencer, the shots sounded like two hard knocks on a wooden door. The first shot hit Bella in the left shoulder. The second shot found home in the right side of her chest. She stepped back, bumping against the wall before sliding down until her rear hit the floor.

Time became immeasurable. The world wobbled, tilting on its axis like a ship out at sea during a storm. When Kristy came back into view, she held a red container and was throwing some liquid all over the room. She turned to Bella, who now smelled the stench of gasoline.

"Sorry, Bella. It's the hunt, you know? It's hard to satisfy."

Kristy walked toward the door, turned, and lit a match. She tossed it on the bed, which burst into flames. The yellow, orange, and red inferno blazed. As the smoke filled Bella's lungs, causing her to cough, spikes of pain ripped through her upper body. She wasn't angry at her friends. She looked at Sienna's corpse and then at the red container Kristy had left behind. They'd both been right.

A lioness had to hunt.

Bella just never expected to become the prey.

***

Duke's Birthday Bash

by Robert Smith

The Second Secretary of the British Embassy was by the front desk of the Hyatt Regency Capitol Hill conducting a thorough examination of a fern. He was a bit of a potted plant himself. Bannon was about 5'6", on the paunchy side, with a broad open face, ruddy, light brown hair and small watery clueless eyes. A fine specimen of that breed of Englishman had once built and sustained empires by any means necessary, and in the 21st century didn't have a fucking clue what to do with themselves. Cowan perused the perfectly cut speckled-gray suit accented with red silk fibers woven into the wool. Quite the swanky wee package was this Bannon.

"Mr. Bunion?" he suggested malevolently, extending his hand.

"It's Bannon," said Bannon. "Bannon."

"Must have written it down wrong."

"A drink perhaps?" Bannon mimed the tipping of a glass while pointing at the bar with his pinky. One of the gestures was redundant, but the man did work for the government. "What's your poison?"

"I'd rather have a coffee."

"I don't think I've ever heard *that* from a Scotsman," Bannon said, elevating an eyebrow.

"How many of us have you met?" Cowan asked. "Two?"

Seemingly under strict instructions to be tolerant, Bannon slapped a toothy smile across the moonscape of his face. His eyes didn't change at all though. He was going to be solicitous as a mortician and as much use to Cowan as a wooden compass.

Inside the West Wing Café the lighting was low-key and the map of the Chesapeake Bay behind the creamer bucket resembled an angry blue dragon.

93

Bannon demanded of the barista an elaborate mocha latte concoction would have confounded the expertise of Dr. Frankenstein in his laboratory and folded the receipt carefully, like he was started making an origami crane. It must have been a recoverable expense. They sat at a window table. Tourists wandered by outside, looking lost, fingers pecking at their map apps, which weren't helping. Once humans had only needed to know the location of the sun. Mind you, that had been a hell of an issue in Glasgow.

Cowan nodded at the foaming cup. "Six dollars for that? That's daylight robbery. What's in it? Ambrosia, nectar of the Gods?"

Bannon dipped his long spoon so as not to disturb the chocolate swirl. "It's my understanding that while here you'll only be. . ."

"Seeing the sights."

"Because what we wouldn't want is. . ."

"Any bother."

"I think, from our perspective, what we'd like is bother kept to an absolute minimum, yes?" Bannon studied him. "You're not here about the Teresa Neele business then?"

"Who's she when she's at home?"

"Detective Inspector . . ."

"I promise to watch my step and not get in trouble and insult nobody and leave town in a week without any bother and make your job smooth as butter hunky-dory and nice and easy does it, old chap."

Bannon blinked at him like a broken machine.

Cowan crossed his heart. "Scout's honor."

"You were a scout?"

"Hell no. Didn't want to get myself buggered by one of them English scoutmasters. Boy's Brigade. Way safer."

"It would be for the best," Bannon declaimed grimly, "to stay far away from George Washington and the girl's former classmates and Professors and so forth, yes?"

"Is George Washington still alive?"

Bannon's face looked like a jellyfish in a string bag

By the Capitol, a reporter in a red coat addressed a semicircle of cameras. Either that or Little Red Riding Hood was giving a press conference. There were wolves in D.C. right enough. Cowan skipped the Metro, thinking a walk on such a brisk day would clear his head. He was at the Constitution Gardens within sight of the Lincoln Memorial before he turned north. People walked quickly like ants running home with something. He chucked a quarter into an upturned cap and a homeless man with an earmuff secured by scotch tape nodded deranged approval.

On 21st Street a girl strolled by wearing a harness from which four fishing lines rose to a cluster of red balloons. A wireless camera suspended from the balloons. Cowan hoped it was performance art. Turning along H Street he saw two students having difficulty unchaining a bicycle from a rack. Sometimes he had cause to question evolution. There was construction all around GW, cranes tilting across the skyline above pyramids of yet to be laid drainpipes and coils of cable. Cement mixers churned. Drills drilled. Hammers hammered. He arrived at the entrance of Rome Hall accidentally. He'd heard that all roads led to Rome.

Cowan consulted the directory in the lobby and took the elevator to the third floor. Sheppard's office door was closed. The posted hours were for a Thursday.

There was a secretary in the office. She was in her late 40's, African-American, preoccupied. She had a complex weave designed to hide the damage done by too many years of the hot comb. Her face was lined, but it looked like she'd got that way having fun at least. Her eyes were baby round and of the same blue as her jeans.

"Hi," he said. She looked startled, being used to dealing with a younger clientele. "I'm looking for Professor Sheppard?"

"He only comes in Thursdays," she said, appraising him.

"Man's only in one day a week? What kind of job is that? There's the work I want."

"You said it," she said, smiling. "He only got one class a semester. His *seminar*."

She pronounced *seminar* the same way she would *shitpile*. Her nameplate said Connie Williams. Connie wasn't a fan of the Professor.

"Nice work if you can get it."

"Where's your accent from?" she asked.

"Same place as me. Glasgow. Scotland."

She looked at him with interest. "My nephew married a girl from Edinburgh. She sound just like you."

"Been there?"

"No," she said, sadly. "I'd like to. In all those books when a woman goes visit she meets some man in a kilt and he always fine and he always sweep her off her feet. You know how they do?"

"Aye, young lassies like you cannot resist your kilted highlander. You know what those boys wear under it don't you?"

She smiled flirtatiously. "I heard it ain't nuthin'."

"Naw, that's a myth. You Americans believe anything you're told. They wear a smaller kilt. And under that another one smaller still."

She was laughing now.

"There's dozens of them. It's a whole big Russian doll situation, only with kilts."

"Where's yours?"

"Dry cleaners. Had to get dried blood out of it. It's enough to make you think about not using a claymore anymore."

A bearded graduate student in sandals came in with an inquiry about a jammed photocopier. He looked at them oddly, having overheard part of the conversation.

Cowan rested his elbow on a filing cabinet. "But you should visit. The lads will be freaking out when they see you. Scottish lassies have way too much body hair. They look like Yetis. Seriously. It's a thing.

In high school I got off with one looked like Sasquatch."

"We had a lovely girl on exchange here last year from Scotland," Connie said. " I don't know if you heard about that? The one went missing?"

"Do you have a number for this Sheppard? Or does he spend the rest of his week on a beach in the Seychelles?"

Connie leaned in, confidentially. "He's in there now, conferencing. With the door closed. Which is a big no-no these days. We're not supposed to let anyone know he's here. Unofficial office hours."

"Maybe I'll knock on his door, unofficially like."

"If you want I can call ahead."

"No. It'll be a nice surprise. I'm sure a writer likes surprises."

"Not that one," she offered, with a sneer.

Cowan pressed his ear to the door. Then he rapped on it. There was a scuffling inside. He knocked again, harder.

"Yes," called a nervous voice. "What is it?"

"Professor Sheppard," Cowan shouted. "Can you come out to play?"

The door opened and the slightly disheveled Professor stood in the frame with a demeanor appropriate to a cornered rodent. He was smallish, pale and reed-thin with a fledgling beard, un-tucked long-sleeved red-striped Brooksgate button-down shirt, and unlaced Timberland boots. He wore a scarlet bandanna also. Maybe he aspired to be a Mexican gangster. His jean buckle belt was missing a front loop.

"Can I help you?" Sheppard attempted a smile, failed. "This is not an office hour."

"I have some questions about Teresa Neele. If you have a minute."

Sheppard's expression mutated from mild annoyance to serious regret. He looked Cowan over like he was a marked down flannel shirt. "Oh, just wait a second," he said. "I have to get finished up with a student."

97

He closed the door. Taped to it was the jacket of his last novel, solitary barn against hellish skyline. *Southern noir. . .despair-filled, hickory-smoked, swamp-damp literature echoing the matter-of-fact cynicism of Cormac McCarthy and the conspicuous immorality of Jim Thomson. Jim Sheppard has looked in the abyss and writes like the devil was after him.*

Well he was now.

The door reopened. Typical faculty office, narrow, bookshelves high on the wall either side, packed tight and over-spilling, suggesting how the weight of narrative could become an avalanche. More books scattered on chairs and desk like a fungoid growth. A couple of soft chairs upholstered in yellow. Ranged on the desk a brown-stained coffee cup, a metal water bottle, a black phone with a twisted and knotted wire, a Munch's scream doll, a stapler, shoe polish tin full of paper clips. The smallish cake with centered candle was out of place. So was Sheppard, who looked like a ferret had got up his trouser leg.

The girl who had opened the door was tanned and chunky, with a thick mane of honey blonde hair. She looked flushed and mussed, but not embarrassed. Maybe she thought this douche a notch on her own belt. You never knew what a nineteen-year-old was thinking. Sometimes they just weren't engaged in that fatiguing process at all. She saw Cowan looking at the cake.

"It's Duke's birthday," she explained.

"Were you giving him a present? In my day we used to bring teachers apples."

"We were conferencing," Sheppard said, hoarsely. "Jill's a talented writer."

"What you writing about, Jill?"

The question seemed to unsettle her. She tried to make eye contact with Sheppard, but he had begun an intricate study of the Poe bobblehead on his radiator.

"I have to go do that thing," Jill said. In one fluid motion she was up, offered the room a mouthful of teeth and darted to the door. It took all her self-control not to break into a sprint in the corridor.

"They have a lot of energy at that age. Places to be. People to do."

"How can I help you?"

"I wanted to ask you about Teresa. I'm here on her family's behalf. If that's O.K.?"

"Of course. I can't imagine how hard it must be for her family."

"I'd imagine you could imagine it," Cowan said. "You being a writer. Isn't that what they call empathy?"

Sheppard made a miniscule adjustment in his bandanna.

"So you two didn't get along that well?"

Sheppard had a quick scratch at his little soul patch. "Where did you hear that?"

"I keep my ear to the ground." Cowan leaned back and smiled. "You must keep your ear to the ground too."

"Being a writer?"

"Being so short."

Sheppard dropped his elbows on the desk. He clasped his hands together, fretful.

"This is a great setup," Cowan said, looking around. "Teach one class, no office hours. You have a place in the Hamptons as well?"

"I can see you're upset."

"That's dead observant. That's what must make you a writer. Being observant. Must come in handy when you're writing about your swamps and dwarves and southern crackers buggering sheep or whatever the hell it is you do."

Sheppard's eyes iced over. "Who did you say you were again?"

"I didn't. This class she was in with you. Could you give me a roster?"

Connie poked her head round the door. "Oh, Duke. I didn't know you were in. Everything alright?"

"It's fine," Sheppard hissed through gritted teeth. "We'll talk about it later." He called her back in. "Could you bring my lunch? Back of the refrigerator in the office?"

99

"Duke?" Cowan sneered. "Seriously?"

Sheppard ignored him. "It was a very exclusive writing seminar. You apply to get in. You need a strong writing sample. Teresa has talent. Had."

Connie returned with a plastic container. Sheppard took the lid off. It was some tofu concoction. She hadn't closed the door.

"What's that?" Cowan asked. "Looks like fungus."

"It's actually very good."

"So, a copy of that roster then and I'll be out of what's left of your hair?"

"I'm sorry," Sheppard said, forking the white rubber in his mouth. It was like he was eating tiny pieces of elastic band. "That's contrary to what I can do. That's covered by FERPA. College privacy regulations, and so on."

"No-one would know if you slipped us a copy but."

Sheppard dabbed his mouth with a napkin. "Worth more than my job's worth."

"How much is that?" Cowan asked. "You do all right. No teaching. Screwing dumb wee co-eds. That a fringe benefit?"

"I'm going to have to ask you to leave," Sheppard said, getting to his feet. "I've had quite enough of this."

Cowan stood too. He walked to the door, closed it and came back.

"Wait a minute," Sheppard yelped. "Who do you think you are?"

"I'm the man's going to put you in the infirmary, fuckface."

Cowan grabbed Sheppard by the scruff of the neck and slammed him face down into the tofu container. He held him there as he choked, suffocating on the stuff. It was a cholesterol free death at any rate.

"Still good?"

Sheppard made a panicked snuffling noise and his fingers scrabbled desperately on the desk. Cowan put his full weight across the man's back. When he at last pulled him out, gasping and flailing, he jammed his nose up hard against the computer screen. Wet stringy snot on the pixels now.

"What I need you to do is to call up that roster."

"I can't do that. . . . I . . ."

Cowan swept the tofu container off the desk. He ripped the candle out the cake. "Dessert?"

This time it was into his own birthday cake that he plunged Sheppard's face, his nostrils and mouth deep-sixed in cream cheese, submerged in marzipan. He sputtered, drowning in sweetness, blacking out on sugar, falling down a deep dark chocolate well.

"See," Cowan whispered. "Who says you can't have your cake and eat it too?"

He extracted the Professor from the cake and thrust his head back against the screen. Sticky icing gummed his eyelashes shut. Cowan tore off the man's stupid bandanna and wiped the splurge away with it.

"Why no picture of this one?" he said, pointing at the screen.

"She was odding," Sheppard mumbled. His nose was bleeding.

Cowan smacked him on the temple with his elbow. "Ice cream giving you a brain freeze, dipshit?"

"She was auditing," Sheppard sputtered. "She's not a regular student. I let her in because she's so good."

"At what? Fellatio?" Cowan began cramming the bandanna into the man's mouth. "Honestly, I think I've heard quite enough from you."

The Professor made muffled crying noises, a strand of saliva dripped on the desk.

"Print it." Cowan commanded. "Where does it come out?"

Sheppard nodded at the door. "Wa Wawa."

"The office? Fair enough. Thanks, Duke. It's been an education." Cowan dragged the man's contorted face up to his own, the bandanna protruding like a huge tongue from his mouth. "By the way, if you leave in the next ten minutes I'm going to come back and chop your tiny dick off. Got it?"

Sheppard's teeth were grinding together squeakily. "Ah Wawawa."

101

Cowan retrieved the roster from the office photocopier.

"Oh," Connie said, surprised. "He actually helped you."

"That's one menacing person," Cowan said, giving a little shiver. "I can see how come he writes all that dark stuff."

"Really?"

They began laughing.

"Seriously, Connie, I think you could knock him down with your eyelashes."

"He's quite a hit with our female students," she said. "Go figure."

"Aye, you'd suppose that one couldn't pay a drunk monkey to go interfering with him. Listen, I'm sending you a postcard when I get back with a list of eligible kilted bachelors want to marry a naïve young U.S. lass."

Connie blushed. "Only if they got big estates. That's my dealbreaker."

"Every one will be a laird or a marquis." Cowan was whispering now. "By the by, a Professor is going to come belting in here in ten minutes time screaming bloody murder and asking for the police. I'll be frank with you. There was an altercation. It involved tofu."

Connie shrugged.

"And cake."

"You been a bad boy?"

"Aye, I have. Should I shove a book down the back of my trousers? Am I due a spanking?" He winked. "I wish."

"I don't switch little kids don't know no better," Connie said, giggling. "I'll be sure campus security knows where not to find you. That ain't no thing. Just hope you didn't go hurting him too little."

Cowan pointed both forefingers at her. "I'm upgrading you to Viscount or Earl."

*

Cowan walked back along the mall towards the Capitol. The 52 miles of scaffolding wrapped around the white dome gave it a spiky appearance. American democracy was under repair.　He stopped outside Kogod's on New Jersey Avenue to send a text to Bannon.

"Hey," it began.　"I'm in a wee bit of bother."

Pulp Modern

Vol. 2 No. 1   May 2017

Mark David Adam

Calvin Demmer

Myke Edwards

L.S. Engler

Marc E. Fitch

Adam S. House

Lucy Kiff

Nick Manzolillo

Mario E. Martinez

Stephen D. Rogers

Joseph Rubas

Tim P. Walker

Michaël Wertenberg

Editor: Alec Cizak

Current and past issues available at online booksellers

Read the Anthony-nominated, high octane series called,
"Masterful, exciting and obliquely funny." (Booklist)

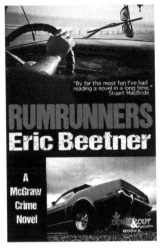

'My favorite book of 2015 has to be
RUMRUNNERS by Eric Beetner, by far the most
fun I've had reading a novel in a long time.
Stuart MacBride, author of the Logan McRae series

"Buckle up...Rumrunners is a fast and furious
read."
Samuel W. Gailey, author of Deep Winter

"Rumrunners just never lets up. It's a
fuel-injected, mile-a-minute thrill ride.
I had a blast."
Grant Jerkins, author of A Very Simple Crime

"Fast, furious & craftful. Recommended."
Sean Doolittle, author of The Cleanup

"Characters display unexpected but plausible depths,
and Beetner effectively balances action scenes with
quieter moments."
Publishers Weekly

Anthony Award nominee - best paperback original

"No padding here, no bouts of introspection. Just good
writing and straight ahead storytelling at a relentless pace."
Booklist

"Characters as rich and lively as any Elmore Leonard novel."
Brian Panowich, author of Like Lions and Bull Mountain

"Eric Beetner is already miles ahead of the competition, but
in Leadfoot he's found yet another gear."
Allan Guthrie, author of Hard Man and Savage Night

"A hell of a fun book. Fast, funny and thrilling on a
classic level."
Steph Post, author of Lightwood

"A terrific book. 0 to 60 in 3 seconds."
Joe Ide, author of I.Q.

QUICK
&
DIRTY

FLASH ⚡ **FICTION**

FLASH ⚡ **FICTION**

FL **SH** ⚡ **FICTION**

SH ⚡ **FICTION**

SH ⚡ **FICTION**

SH ⚡ **FICTION**

SH ⚡ **FICTION**

Ride On

by JL Boekestein

"I don't want you to fuck up my rides," Tyler told Brendan when he started driving limos. "Fuck up and I'll break your bones and kick you out on the street. *Comprendre*?"

"Comprende boss," Brendan replied. *Don't fuck up.*

He didn't fuck up. Never.

All kinds rented a limo. Funerals, weddings, frat boys, celebrities (real or wannabees), businessmen, businessmen with hookers (those were the best tippers). Brendan drove and provided other services. You needed something? Tickets to games or a show, something to snort, blow or shoot? Something to fuck? Brendan knew how to arrange things, how to smooth out little or bigger problems. Anything, you just asked Brendan.

Yes, the clients liked Brendan driving them around.

And he liked driving them around. He liked the work and the money.

So it wasn't fair when Brendan was gunned down when was holding the door of the limo for some real estate guy with shady connections. It was in front of the Hilton. The fucking Hilton!

The guy died. Brendan ended up in hospital.

And out of hospital again. The insurance for limo drivers sucked. Really sucked.

Alone at home. No job, not with that leg. Nobody, he hadn't needed anybody ever.

He had pain killers, plenty of them.

You could see it coming from a mile away. In a year Brendan wouldn't be doing pain killers, he would be doing other shit. Bad shit. His money would evaporate, he would lose his place, he would be doing petty crime and die on the street, or end up in jail.

Miles and miles away. As clear as snow on a glass table top.

*

107

Perez picked up the guy at his hotel. Suit, gold rimmed glassed, bling time piece, rings. A player. And he gave Perez a c-note for opening the car door.

"Thank you Mr. Taylor."

"What's your first name, son? I haven't seen you before."

"Perez, sir. I am new."

"Perez, tonight I'm gonna have the best time of my life. You're the guy who can drive me there?"

"I sure can, Mr. Taylor."

"Good, first get me to a place where a guy can pick up a few dates. Boobs and ass, but classy. A few girls ready for a party in town."

"I know just the place, Mr. Taylor."

Perez phoned Madame Chen. She had the best girls.

While Mr. Taylor nailed some flesh, Perez waited on the parking lot, in the limo.

A blond girl came over, with the compliments of Mr. Taylor. If he could be ready in the hour.

Perez was.

Booze, broads and coke. Perez drove Mr. Taylor and his two dates—a beautiful redhead and some gorgeous ebony chick—all over town. Dancing, gambling, a *tits and ass show.* "Join us, Perez. Otherwise Macy has no-one to talk to." Macy was the redhead.

Fuck, damn. Mr. Taylor knew how to have a good time, and he wasn't stingy either. Benjamin Franklins, all of them.

One of those nights the other guys bragged about. Yeah, like those things really happened.

With Mr. Taylor they did.

They ended up watching the sun rise at that Hot Dog place Perez didn't even know existed. After dropping of the girls at Madame Chen's Mr. Taylor had insisted on having breakfast.

"Best damn chili dogs in town," Mr. Taylor said in between two bites. "The perfect ending of a fucking great night."

Perez agreed. They were.

Back in the limo, with the window between them down, Mr. Taylor put five hundred dollar in Perez' hands. "That is the last of them. Thanks for the good time, Perez. And you keep quiet about them. Tell, me is Tyler is still an ass?"

"I..." If he couldn't trust I guy who had tipped him over two grant during the night, who could he trust? "Yeah, he is."

Mr. Taylor nodded. From his pocket he took a nickel plated revolver. Such a small thing, but still a gun.

"You can tell him Brendan said 'hi'. And good luck with that credit card I charged this night on."

Without saying anything else Brendan put the gun against his head and blew his brains out, fucking up Tyler's best limo.

Finally.

***

The Price of a Burger

by Richard Risemberg

For reasons you don't need to know about, I was running around the night with my hair done up in pink-frosted blond curls, gelled into little cat claws all over my head. I am normally a regular-looking guy, and I didn't change clothes or anything; I needed to look clueless for the business at hand. The business was done now, and I'd survived, but after I got back into my car I had the shakes. You know how they start up afterward, even when you think you've been Mr. Cool. So I headed onto the big empty freeway and started to drive off my nerves.

I found my way to the Hollywood Freeway and rode toward the gap in the hills that led to the "Movie Capital of the World," where they kept the flow of dog food commercials, fistfight dramas, and cheap laughs spilling into the American swamp unabated. I crested the ridge in darkness, and the wind of my own motion whistled in the open windows of the car. It was only a minute before I saw the offramp into Hollywood and edged towards it.

I'm not sure why I didn't just go home. Maybe I'd read too many Didion novels. I joined the traffic jam of taxis, tour buses, and rental cars and looked at the famous shit outside my windows. Souvenir shops, fake museums, and pornographic bookstores: this was what the world aspired to, and spent their money to visit. There was a parking space in front of a shabby burger stand. I pulled into it reflexively. A parking space to an LA driver is like a line at a grocery store to

110

a hungry Russian: you just go for it. I supposed I should eat something. The burger stand was narrow, loud, and full of punk rockers. I held my blond-dyed head up high and marched in. The air smelled of old grease and cigarettes. The music was loud. No one bothered to notice me. It was perfect.

I sat at the counter. The only menu was one of those backlit plastic boards with slots for cheap black capital letters. Every item was misspelled, most likely on purpose. Nothing seemed appetizing, but I had to eat. The counter girl came up to me. She had a shaved head and a big red heart tattooed onto her cheek. The heart bore the legend "Kafka" in lowrider script. I bet she knew how to spell all right. She smiled at my hair and asked what I wanted. I told her I didn't know, and she said, "Coming right up," and smiled again. Her smile showed a broken tooth. I played along and waited for my food. I'm still not sure what it was, but I wouldn't recommend it. It plopped into my gut like so many road apples. A beer showed up next to my plate, and I drank it. What the hell. I didn't live in the Movie Capital of the World for nothing.

A girl of the *Waif,/Scrawny* category sat down on the stool next to mine. She nudged me with her elbow and asked if she could touch my hair. I said to go ahead, and she did. Her own hair looked like it had been styled by an eggbeater, but who was I to talk at that moment. She shouted "Cool!" over the thrash of guitars coming out of the loudspeakers. I smiled at her, and she smiled back. It was a pretty desperate smile. Someone else grabbed at my arm and pulled me around on the barstool. A skinny punk kid with hair bleached blonder than mine glowered at me from

111

behind a network of tattoos. He had more graffiti on his face than a lot of back-alley fences.

"Bitch! You trying to hit on my girl? Bitch!" He moved his face up close to mine. I smelled a set-up. I slid off the barstool and stood up. While I am by no means a bruiser, at six feet and 180 I'm not fragile either. He didn't back off. The punk's head came up to about my nose, so I stood up straighter to make sure he wouldn't head-butt me. Just then a pair of arms came around me and pinned my own arms to my sides. The punk grinned. I did the only thing I could think of at the moment and pushed back hard, mashing whoever had grabbed me against the hard edge of the counter. I heard a faint squeak over the music, and the arms let go of me. This gave me a little room, so I kept my weight back, lifted my leg, and kicked Mr. Aggro in the chest. It wasn't an elegant kick, it wasn't even a real kick, more like a shove, but it propelled him backwards through the open door of the burger joint, backpedaling frantically to keep from falling. He would have been better off falling. Instead, he flailed into three Marines who were walking down the boulevard, knocking one of them into the gutter. The other two turned into scowling masks under their high-and-tight haircuts, and each grabbed one of Mr. Aggro's arms and dragged him out of view. The third Marine pushed himself out of the gutter, looking wet and furious. I turned around to deal with whoever had grabbed me. It was the girl who had admired my hair, and she was crying. I left her alone. I asked the shaven-headed counter girl for the bill, and she shouted, "It's on the house. I hope those two cockroaches never come back. Now get out before it gets worse."

It was the most reasonable thing I'd heard all day. I got back in the car and headed home. The shakes were long gone. I checked the rearview, and saw a couple of motor cops ride right up onto the sidewalk where the Marines were still at work. I don't know why, but I started whistling.

***

© 2017 Richard Risemberg

Modern Samurai

by Mike Loniewski

There was a panic in the corporate lobby of
Schwizer Firearms, a weapons conglomerate perched
atop a modern Berlin high rise. Sitting perfectly calm
through screaming and smoke were Reiko Masamune
and a stunned Schwizer attorney named Gebhard
whose head resembled a bespectacled potato. They
let the shock of the blast subside, and the haze clear
through the stream of sprinklers showering down.
Pieces of shattered doors lay at their feet. There was
something that looked like a foot in a fine dress shoe.
It had been a bomb, and Reiko had put it there.

"I think they'll see me, now," she said to Gebhard,
pointing to ground zero.

The meager lump of a man swallowed hard. This
was outrageous. He was under the notion she had
arrived to supply signatures forfeiting her portion of the
company, not blow up Schwizer executives, which had
now become violently apparent.

"Perhaps I should excuse myself?" he asked.

"Oh, no," said Reiko, flipping the locks on her
briefcase.

From it rose a fully loaded Masamune submachine
gun with an extended magazine, a gun that her family
had perfected over centuries of weapon
craftsmanship, now gone in a sweeping betrayal of
business and blood that put Masamune's storied
history into Schwizer's hands and a poison into her
father's veins.

She winked at Gebhard. "You're the mediator,
now. You're going to help bring this to a peaceful
resolution."

Of all the threats to a massive fortune five hundred
company, a sleek woman in business dress and heels
holding a submachine gun was low on the list. Yet,
here she was, gliding through the sprinklers, a

waddling attorney as her date. She was here to cut it all down.

Employees at Schwizer were expected to be students of the company. Executives insisted that knowledge of their product was paramount and that all workers, no matter their role, were expected to pack heat. They lived by their products. They died by their products. Old Gebhard was strapped.

The little chode held a Schwizer .45 Tactical and placed Reiko between its ergonomic sights. The truth in how skilled a shooter Gebhard was lay in how he held the weapon, as if it were a dead animal plucked from the grass.

He pulled the trigger with a flinch and the bullet skimmed across the side of Reiko's skull. She fell forward, her gun and briefcase sliding across the wet floor. Gebhard inched close to inspect his handiwork, craning his neck for a glimpse of the wound. Gebhard had never shot a living thing. There was guilt, and a bit of pride. He was a hero. His wife may even reward him with a blowjob. Gebhard the warrior.

A knife plunged through the top of Gebhard's pudgy foot, a double edged instrument of steel from Reiko Masamune that cut tendon and bone. He howled and fell to the floor. Reiko twisted out the knife and held the blade to the stacks of flesh that made up his neck.

"Is this going to be indicative of our relationship?" asked Reiko, blood streaming from her wound and staining her face like war paint.

Gebhard managed a whimper as a hot wet stain spread across the front of his trousers. By his tie, Reiko dragged him into the wreckage of the boardroom.

Inside, standing amongst shattered glass and splintered furniture, Reiko handed Gebhard a document. Ensuring that her family's company would never remain in Schwizer's hands was her first priority. The men who plotted the takeover lay in pieces around her, except one.

115

"A bomb," muttered Helmuth Schwizer, president of Schwizer Firearms. "You used a goddamn bomb."

Reiko sneered at the odious man. "I couldn't resist."

"Congratulations," said Helmuth. "You'll be remembered as a terrorist."

"No. A ronin."

Reiko turned to Gebhard. "I'm sure there was a vote," she said. "Whatever the result, it's now ash. You're to record the board's new vote, ten to nothing in favor of the dissolution of Schwizer Firearms."

She wound up and kicked Helmuth in his ribs. "All we need is a motion from dear Helmuth."

She crouched down to him. "Mr. Schwizer," said Reiko. "Would an autograph out of the question?"

"Give me that document. I'll piss on it."

Reiko's eyes snaked a trail down Helmuth's wounded body. She found a jagged gash in along his leg, raw and open. Her double edged knife probed the shrapnel wound and Helmuth let out a horrible scream of mercy.

"Sounds like you're reconsidering," said Reiko. "Are we making progress?"

Helmuth shook his head violently in the affirmative. With a bloodied hand, he scribbled his signature for the motion and pushed the document away.

"It'll never hold in court," he sneered.

"He's right," said Gebhard. "I can't see this being regarded as legitimate, Miss Masumune."

"You're loyal, Gebhard," Reiko observed. "If you read closely, Mr. Schwizer will reward you specifically for that loyalty. If you ensure his wishes for the company are met without interference, that is."

Gebhard skimmed the document and his eyes widened down the page. "Indeed I will," he said as he turned and limped off.

Helmuth managed a wet chuckle. "Clever bitch."

Reiko pointed to the far wall where behind a shattered display case sat a gleaming katana of precisely tempered steel.

116

"You hung it," she said of her family's legacy. "Like some hunter's trophy."

"You and your father believing that sword ever held any meaning is the saddest thing I've had to watch."

Reiko tiptoed through the gore and removed the sword from the shattered case. It felt heavy, as if the collective dishonor of her ancestors was pressed into her hand.

Helmuth snickered. "I suppose you're gonna kill me with it? Dad's final wish?"

Reiko raised her submachine gun. "No. Dad made me promise to kill you with his gun."

She squeezed the trigger until the magazine emptied and pieces of Helmuth were missing.

For a moment she gripped the sword hoping to feel the hands of her ancestors who held it before her. Then she opened her blouse and dragged the great sword across her abdomen and felt the wave of honor she was fighting for. She smiled as her blood ran down the blade and soaked into the woven handle leaving her own indelible mark on its legacy.

***

Baggage

Joe Ricker

Sarah waited for the slightest fade in the darkness outside, when that first hint of blue pushed up from the horizon, before she crept away from his puttered breathing. All the things she needed were already in place. Her shorts at the hamper, ID and cash in the pockets. Her purse on the chair near the door, and her keys to the Audi parked on the street were exactly where she would leave them—in plain sight of him, if he woke up. She made an arc through the house, moving on the balls of her feet, grabbed the shorts, a yellow shirt and a cap hung on a hook near the door in the kitchen.

She'd come into the life she was leaving with an adoration for the way he'd spoken and touched her, his lips against her ear lobe, his fingers a light, almost secret brush against her face. After time, his distance from her ear grew until there was silence, and the pressure of his knuckles left its echo on her flesh. Outside, she crossed the street to the narrow space between her neighbors' homes. She stopped and pulled a bag of garbage from a trashcan and retrieved her wheeled luggage.

*

The sun throws a thin arm of light over the ledge of the horizon, bringing faint color to dim houses. Hours before, when it was still dark, Mr. Wax climbed into the back of the car they would wait in—an Impala with sticky cloth seats that they picked up at the airport when they dropped off the last rental. Mr. Wax didn't fly, and airports were the only place to get one-way rentals. They'd been moving south from Chicago— Indianapolis, St. Louis, Memphis, New Orleans. Four cities in four days, sinking deeper into the rising heat, trading cars in each new city.

Sheldon slides over behind the wheel and watches the sun poke its head into the sky—the radiance of

118

accomplishment. He was half asleep when they got there. He doesn't remember what street they're on, only that they made a turn off Magazine, and then more of them until Mr. Wax parked in front of a pink house with Mardi Gras beads draped over the points of a wrought-iron fence. The street is residential, quiet, much different than the back alleys near the bars they'd lurked before.

This job was special, Mr. Wax had told him.

A layer of sweat clings to Sheldon's white polo shirt. *Wear simple, plain clothes,* Mr. Wax instructed. *Inconspicuous. Leave your wallet and anything that can identify you,* he said after asking if Sheldon had any tattoos. He didn't. Mr. Wax's faint snoring from the back seat gives Sheldon a sense of comfort, like there's a level of respect for his abilities even though Mr. Glenn, Mr. Wax's boss, only ever let Sheldon pick up dry-cleaning or run packages to the poker rooms— when they called him *Paperweight or Notsobright* or *Special* instead of his name.

The heat is heavy and dense around him. Sweat on his body feels like a layer of skin he could peel away. *Heat*, he remembers. Mr. Glenn talked about that with Mr. Wax before they left. He'd said: *Heat is increasing, and people are getting sloppy. It's time for them to cool off. Head South. Clean up and dump the baggage in New Orleans.* They chose Sheldon because no one would see him coming. He could get close.

The only motion on the street is a woman, and Sheldon doesn't see her until long after the wheels of the carry-on baggage she's dragging over brick grabbed his attention. She rounds the corner—a quick, determined pace. He notices her collar bones most, like daggers she could yank away to pierce anything blocking her path.

He thinks about the three men he's killed along the way, the loud gunshot escorting the bullet to whisper through their brain. A final, rapid lullaby. Sheldon wonders what their last thoughts were. The first guy's stringent cologne nauseated him before the singe of gunpowder chased it away. He'd only ever felt present

119

in life, something without purpose, like a stranger at a party who people whispered about instead of speaking with. Sheldon tries to remember the interstates they took to get there from Chicago.

A tree-of-life medallion dangles from her neck. She has a narrow waist, short white cut-offs. The taper of her thigh muscles flex in striations close to her hips. *Stems*. That's what they call legs like that. The sleeves of her yellow, collared shirt are rolled up over her elbows. She moves closer, ahead of the plastic rumble. Sheldon's heart drums movement into the beads of sweat on his chest. A jittery, warm rush crouches inside him. There's a glint of moisture on her temples, a severe gaze in her blue eyes. The *Costa* trucker-hat she's wearing is pulled low.

Sarah makes it to the corner, the rising sun on her back encouraging her movement. Ahead of her, glints of the sun's light ricochets from shiny particles in the asphalt and the mirrors and thin bands of chrome around windows of the cars she's passing. She wants to check behind her, make sure there's no one following, but that would mean looking back, breaking the first promise she made to herself. She won't look back.

The world has never really made sense to Sheldon, but he wonders in that moment, as he watches the woman pass, about love at first sight—if love can actually happen in milliseconds, less time than it takes for a bullet through the head to kill someone. He's never been in love, never stumbled down that route. He wonders why they chose him. Mr. Wax shifts in the back seat. Sheldon catches movement in the rear-view mirror when he turns back toward the wheel. A sudden electric shudder rolls over him, and Mr. Wax pushes the end of a pistol silencer against his skull.

***

WRITER TYPES
PODCAST

hosted by
Eric Beetner
S.W. Lauden

A crime and mystery fiction podcast
hosted by two Anthony Award
nominated authors

Interviews, book reviews, short fiction & more

Listen in for interviews with: Joe R. Lansdale, Megan Abbott,
Laura Lippman, Reed Farrel Coleman, Lou Berney,
Meg Gardiner, Ryan Gattis, Sara Paretsky Johnny Shaw
and many more!

New episode every month on iTunes, Stitcher & Soundcloud

THE
SIN
TAX

PRESTON LANG

UNTIMELY DEMISE

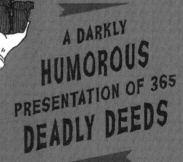

A DARKLY **HUMOROUS** PRESENTATION OF 365 **DEADLY DEEDS**

WILLIAM DYLAN **POWELL**

ILLUSTRATED BY
ALEX KALOMERIS

Author Bios & Acknowledgements

Zakariah Johnson has published in *Shotgun Honey*, *Yellow Mama*, *Sherlock Holmes Mystery Magazine* and elsewhere, and is the cross-genre editor for Folded Word press. His mom once smuggled a switchblade for him out of TJ in her bra: "Miss you, Ma."

Preston Lang is a writer from New York. His work has appeared in *Thuglit, Spinetingler, Crime Syndicate,* and *Betty Fedora.* He also write a regular column for *WebMd*

Charles Roland lives in an area convenient to several major southern cities. His work has appeared in *Workers Write! Tales from the Casino, Mystery Weekly Magazine, Akashic Books' "Mondays are Murder" series, Switchblade Magazine,* and more. He can be reached at charlesrolandauthor.com or charlesrolandauthor@gmail.com.

Eric Beetner is the author of nearly 20 novels and has been called "the 21st century's answer to Jim Thompson." (*Lit Reactor*) He hosts the *Noir at the Bar* reading series in LA, co-hosts the podcast *Writer Types* and has had over 70 short stories published in anthologies and online. ericbeetner.com

J.D. Graves is a recovering playwright who recently fell off the wagon with "TALL PINES LODGE" an official production of the 2016 New York Fringe Festival. His short fiction has appeared in *Near 2 the Knuckle, Intrinsick Magazine,* and more than once in

Noise City Zine. When not writing, he's teaching theatre.

Ehren Baker Having graduated with a B.A. in Literature from the Cal State school system, Ehren "E.A." Baker now pursues publishing his short works, along with novels and poetry. Often playing with themes of mortality, social commentary, and disillusionment, he hopes that his work ultimately explores the human condition in all its absurdities.

Morgan Boyd lives in Santa Cruz California with his wife, daughter, cat, and carnivorous plant collection. He has been published online at *The Flash Fiction Offensive, Shotgun Honey, Near To The Knuckle,* and *Fried Chicken and Coffee.* He also has stories forthcoming at *Tough* and *Yellow Mama.*

Rob McClure Smith is an expat Scot exiled to the cornfields of the Midwest. His fiction has appeared in *Barcelona Review, Manchester Review, Gutter, Chicago Quarterly Review* and other magazines. He's currently working on "The Throne of The Third Heaven", a novel about the misadventures of a hardboiled Glaswegian detective investigating a murder in Washington D.C.

Calvin Demmer is a dark fiction author. His work has appeared in *Bards and Sages Quarterly, Empyreome Magazine, Mad Scientist Journal, Ravenwood Quarterly,* and others. When not writing, he is intrigued by that which goes bump in the night and the sciences of our universe. You can find him online at www.calvindemmer.com or follow him on Twitter @CalvinDemmer.

J. L. Boekestein is an award winning Dutch writer of science fiction, fantasy, horror, thrillers and whatever takes his fancy. He usually writes his stories in trains, coffeehouses and in the 16th century taverns of his native The Hague, the Netherlands. Over the years he has made his living as a bouncer, working for a detective agency and as an editor. Currently he works for the Dutch Ministry of Security and Justice. His English publications include stories in: *Cyäegha, Nonbianary Review, Strange Shifters*, *Lovecraft after Dark*, *Surreal Nightmares*, *Urban Temples of Cthulhu*, *Sirens Call*, *Mystery Weekly Magazine*, *Double Feature Magazine*, *After The Happily Ever After, Cliterature*, *No Safe Word*, *Sex & Sorcery 3* and *Brave Boy World: A Transman Anthology*. http://jlboekestein.wixsite.com/jaap-boekestein

Richard Risemberg was dragged to Los Angeles as a child, and has been working there in a number of vernacular occupations since his teens while writing poetry, articles, essays, and fiction, editing online 'zines, sneaking around with a camera trying to steal people's souls, and making a general nuisance of himself, which is his forte. He's survived long enough to become either a respected elder or a tedious old fart, depending on your point of view, and is still at it. It hasn't been easy for any of us.

Michael Loniewski is a writer from New Jersey. His fiction has been published by *One Eye Press, Shotgun Honey, Out of the Gutter,* and *Big Pulp*. His comics have been published with *Image Comics* and *APE Entertainment*. You can find him on twitter at @redfox_write.

Joe Ricker is a former bartender for Southern literary legends Barry Hannah and Larry Brown. A former cab driver, acquisitions specialist, lumberjack and professor, Ricker now spends his time on the road. His short story collection "Walkin' After Midnight" was published in 2015 and received praise from Ace Atkins, Tom Franklin, Gerry Boyle and Carla Norton.

Special Thanks: to **Rick West**, owner of *Battery Books* in Pasadena, cover model **Zera Vaughan**, and **S.W. Lauden,** host of *Writer Types* podcast, for their continued promotion and support of *Switchblade*.

Made in the USA
San Bernardino, CA
19 October 2017